Brander Matthews

# Introduction to the Study of American Literature

Brander Matthews

**Introduction to the Study of American Literature**

ISBN/EAN: 9783741187094

Manufactured in Europe, USA, Canada, Australia, Japa

Cover: Foto ©Andreas Hilbeck / pixelio.de

Manufactured and distributed by brebook publishing software
(www.brebook.com)

Brander Matthews

**Introduction to the Study of American Literature**

# AN INTRODUCTION

## TO THE STUDY OF

# AMERICAN LITERATURE

BY

## BRANDER MATTHEWS, A.M., LL.B.

PROFESSOR OF LITERATURE IN COLUMBIA COLLEGE

NEW YORK ·:· CINCINNATI ·:· CHICAGO

AMERICAN BOOK COMPANY

INT. TO AM. LIT.

W. P. 4

𝕿𝖔 𝖒𝖞 𝖋𝖗𝖎𝖊𝖓𝖉 𝖆𝖓𝖉 𝕮𝖔𝖑𝖑𝖊𝖆𝖌𝖚𝖊

## NICHOLAS MURRAY BUTLER

DEAN OF THE SCHOOL OF PHILOSOPHY

IN COLUMBIA COLLEGE

# PREFATORY NOTE

THIS book is intended as an introduction to the study of American literature. Although the chapters on the separate authors are wholly distinct, they have been so planned that each of them prepares the way for its successor, and that all of them together outline the changing circumstances under which American literature has developed. An attempt has been made to show how each of the chief American authors influenced his time, and how he in turn was influenced by it; and also to indicate how each of them was related to the others, both personally and artistically.

Bearing in mind the fact that the student needs to have his attention centered on vital points, all dates and all proper names, and all titles of books not absolutely essential, have been rigorously omitted. Interest has thus been concentrated on the literary career of each of the greater writers and on their practice of the literary art, in the hope and expectation that the student will be encouraged and stimulated to read their works for his own pleasure. After the consideration of these more important authors, one by one, the writers of less consequence have been discussed briefly in a single chapter; and in like manner a single chapter only has been devoted to a summary consideration of the condition of our literature at the end of the nineteenth century.

5

To arouse the student's interest in the authors as actual men, the illustrations chosen have been confined to portraits and views, and to facsimiles of manuscripts. To enable him to see for himself the successive stages of the growth of American literature, and to let him discover how the authors sometimes came one after another and sometimes worked side by side, there has been appended also a chronological table of the chief dates in our literary history.

As mere text-book instruction can never be an adequate substitute for the student's own acquaintance with the actual works of the authors discussed, there have been annexed to every chapter bibliographical notes calling attention to the editions most suitable for the student's reading, and also to the best biographies and to a few of the most suggestive criticisms.

The thanks of the author and of the publishers are due to Miss Alice M. Longfellow, Professor Norton, Mr. H. G. O. Blake, Mr. Edward W. Emerson, Mr. Walter R. Benjamin, and Gen. J. G. Wilson, for kindly furnishing the original manuscripts herewith reproduced; to Mr. F. D. Stone, for aid in making a facsimile of Franklin's "Almanac"; and to Dr. Chas. H. J. Douglas of the Brooklyn Boys' High School, for preparing the most of the questions appended to every chapter — questions intended to be suggestive only and by no means exhaustive.

B. M.

# CONTENTS

# LIST OF ILLUSTRATIONS

# AMERICAN LITERATURE

———oo°°oo———

## I  INTRODUCTION

Since the invention of the art of writing, the story of the past is no longer kept alive by word of mouth only, the father telling the son, and the son, in turn, telling the grandson. It has been set down in black and white, by means of letters, so that we to-day can read the record of the feelings, the thoughts, and the acts of the people of two thousand years ago. And we, in our turn, are setting down our sayings and our doings, so that those who come after us will be able to understand what we felt, what we thought, and what we did. When this record is so skill-fully made as to give pleasure to the reader, it is called literature.

Literature, then, is the reflection and the reproduction of the life of the people. It has existed ever since the invention of the art of writing, which enabled men to keep an account of the things they wished to remember. The literature of the past helps us to understand the lives of the peoples of the past. Greek literature tells us how the Greeks lived, and how they felt, what they thought, and what they did. Through Latin literature we get to know the ways of the old Romans ; and, through Hebrew litera-

9

ture, we are enabled to understand the character of the Jewish race.

In like manner, English literature tells us about the life of the peoples who speak the English language. English literature is the record of the thoughts and the feelings and the acts of the great English-speaking race. This record extends a long way back into the past; but it is also being made to-day and every day; and it bids fair to be made for many centuries to come. Greek literature is dead, and Hebrew literature is dead; but English literature is alive now. It is the continuous account of the life of those who speak the English language, in the past, in the present, and in the future. Here in the United States, above the Great Lakes in Canada, across the Atlantic in Great Britain, afar on the other side of the Pacific in Australia and in India, there are now men and women keeping the record of their feelings, their thoughts, and their acts.

All that these men and these women write, if only it be so skillfully presented as to give pleasure to the reader, becomes at once a part of English literature. It is no matter where the authors live, whether in New York or in Montreal, in London, in Melbourne or in Calcutta, what they write in the English language belongs to English literature. It is no matter what the nationality of the author may be, whether he is a citizen of the United States or a subject of the British crown; if he uses the English language he contributes to English literature. This must be remembered always — that the record of the life of the peoples using the English language is English literature.

As literature is a reflection and a reproduction of the life of the peoples speaking the language in which it is written, this literature is likely to be strong and great in proportion as the peoples who speak the language are strong and great.  English literature is therefore likely to grow, as it is the record of the life of the English-speaking race, and as this race is steadily spreading abroad over the globe.

It has been estimated that in the time of Chaucer less than three millions of men and women spoke English, and in the time of Shakspere less than seven millions ; and all these lived in the British Isles.  But after a while the British Isles became too small for those who spoke English. Men and women went east and west out of England, and settled in the four quarters of the earth.  They grew in numbers rapidly.

Another estimate shows that at the beginning of the nineteenth century probably about twenty millions of men and women spoke English, while about thirty-one millions spoke French, and about thirty millions spoke German. Now, at the end of the nineteenth century, it is believed that about fifty millions speak French, and about seventy millions speak German, while more than a hundred and twenty-five millions speak English.  Our language is spreading far more rapidly than any other ; and the prophecy has been made that at the end of the twentieth century the number of those who use the English language will be fully a thousand millions.

While those who speak German are still mostly in Germany, and those who speak French mostly in France, the most of those who speak English are no longer in England, for the total population of all the British Isles is now less than forty millions.  The largest single body of the English-speaking race has not even a political connection with England, for English is the language of the population of the United States, who now number more than sixty millions.  As the people of the United States have vigor and energy and are in no wise inferior to the people of

Great Britain, it seems likely that hereafter the Americans, rather than the British, will be recognized as the chief of the English-speaking peoples.

As long as the English-speaking race dwelt only in the British Isles, English literature had to do only with British subjects. Now that the English-speaking race has settled itself also in America, and now more especially that the chief body of this race is not to be found in the British Isles but in the United States, it is needful to have terms to distinguish that portion of English literature which is written in the British Isles from that which is written in the United States.

Until the Declaration of Independence, the unity of the English race was unbroken; and until the end of the eighteenth century the stream of English literature had but a single channel. Since we in the United States began to have writers of our own, the record of our feelings, of our thoughts, and of our deeds may fairly be called American literature. It is still a part of English literature, for it is written in the English language. As Canada and as Australia are growing and prospering, there can be said to be already a Canadian literature and an Australian literature. And to distinguish the literature of the English-speaking race who continue to live in the British Isles from the literature of the Americans and the Canadians and the Australians, perhaps that had best be called British literature.

So, at the end of the nineteenth century, we find that English literature, one in the past, has now four divisions, — British, American, Canadian, and Australian. Of these, the British is still the most important, having the most great authors. But the American is second to it, and is growing sturdily and steadily. The English literature of the past is as much our glorious heritage as it is that of the British. It belongs to us as it belongs to them, and we have an equal pride in this splendid possession.

But as the American of to-day is unlike an Englishman in many points of custom and of taste, so American literature has begun to differ from British literature in many ways. Literature is a reflection and a reproduction of life, and as life in the United States is more and more unlike life in Great Britain, American literature must needs become more and more unlike British literature. We Americans, for the most part, come of the same stock as the British of to-day, but we have lived, for many generations, in another land, with another climate and under another social organization.

For more than a century now, the American has grown up in a republic free from feudal influences, without caste and class distinctions, with public schools open to rich and poor alike. All these things cannot but have had their effect upon us. We believe that there is a difference between the American and the Englishman — although it is not easy to declare precisely what that difference may be. We believe that there is such a thing as Americanism; and that there have been Americans of a type impossible elsewhere in the world — impossible, certainly, in Great Britain. Washington and Franklin were typical Americans, different as they were; and so were Emerson and Lincoln, Farragut and Lowell. It was Lowell who found in President Hayes "that excellent new thing we call Americanism, which I suppose is that dignity of human nature . . . which consists, perhaps, in not thinking yourself either better or worse than your neighbors by reason of any artificial distinction." This Americanism has left its mark on the writings of the authors of the United States.

It is perhaps for this reason, and perhaps, also, because we all like to find ourselves in the books we read, that American writers are of more interest to us here in the United States than are the recent writers of the other great branch of English literature, the writers now living in the British Isles. British literature reproduces for us a life which is at once like ours, and unlike it. American literature reproduces for us our own life; it records our feelings, our thoughts, and our deeds; it enables us to see ourselves and our neighbors as we really are, or at least as we seem to ourselves to be; it explains us to ourselves. And therefore, even if American literature, which belongs almost wholly to the nineteenth century, were inferior in quality as well as in quantity to the British literature of the nineteenth century, yet it would be of more importance to us here in America. To learn how it came into being and who its founders were ought to be interesting to all of us.

QUESTIONS. — What is literature? Mention several historical divisions of the subject.

Trace the spread of the English-speaking race, from the time of Chaucer to the present day.

How has English literature come to have four geographical divisions?

What is meant by British literature?

What is the distinguishing characteristic of American literature?

NOTE. — There are two primers of American literature, one by Miss Watkins (American Book Company, 35 cents), and one by Prof. C. F. Richardson (Houghton, Mifflin & Co., 50 cents). Prof. Richardson is also the author of a more elaborate work on "American Literature" (G. P. Putnam's Sons, $3.50). Prof. M. C. Tyler has written a history of "American Colonial Literature," of which 4 vols. have now been published (G. P. Putnam's Sons, $6). Very useful is Mr. Whitcomb's "Chronological Outlines of American Literature" (Macmillan & Co., $1.25). Most comprehensive is the "Library of American Literature," edited by Mr. Stedman and Miss Hutchinson (W. R. Benjamin, 11 vols., $33).

## II THE COLONIAL PERIOD

THE English settlements in North America began at a time when English literature had just reached its most glorious period. Shakspere was writing his plays when Captain John Smith first explored Chesapeake Bay. Milton was born the year before Henry Hudson first sailed up the noble river that now bears his name. Bacon published his great book on philosophical and scientific method only a few months before the landing of the Pilgrims on Plymouth Rock.

The men who left England for conscience' sake were many of them scholars with a love for learning. But in this fierce new land in which they sought to establish themselves, they had no time, at first, to do anything more than defend their lives, build their houses, plant their fields, and set up their churches and their schools. They were strong men, laboring mightily, and laying the broad foundations of the republic we live under to-day.

What they wrote then had always an immediate object. They set down in black and white their compacts, their laws, and their own important doings. They described the condition of affairs in the colonies to the kinsfolk and the friends they had left behind in the mother country. They prepared elaborate treatises in which they set forth their own vigorous ideas about religion. For singing songs or for telling tales, they had neither leisure nor taste ; so we find no early American novelist and no early American poet.

Perhaps the beginnings of American literature are to be sought in the books written by the first adventurers for the purpose of giving an account of the strange countries in which they had traveled. Of these adventurers, the most interesting was Captain John Smith. He was born in England in 1579. As a lad, he ran away to become a soldier, and saw much fighting against the Turks. Taken prisoner, he was sold for a slave, but made his escape and went back to England.

In 1607 he was one of those who came over here to found a colony in Virginia. He himself records his being made captive by the Indians, and the saving of his life by Pocahontas, the daughter of the Indian chief, Powhatan. For more than ten years Smith kept coming to America, and exploring the bays and rivers of the coast from Virginia to New England. He published, in 1608, " A True Relation of such Occurrences and Accidents of Note as hath Happened in Virginia," the very first book about any of the English settlements in North America. In 1624 he was one of the authors of " The General History of Virginia, New England, and the Summer Isles." The last years of his life were spent in England, and he died in London in 1632.

John Smith was the most picturesque figure in the early history of America ; and his writings are like him — bold, free, highly colored. He was more picturesque than any of the solid scholars and the stalwart ministers of New England whom we find uniting in the making of what is now known as the " Bay Psalm Book." This was the first English book printed in America. It was published in 1640. Its full title was " The Whole Book of Psalms faithfully Translated into English Metre." The worthy divines who prepared this volume were not born poets ; their verses are halting and their rimes are strained. As it has been said, these hymns "seem to have been hammered out on an anvil, by blows from a blacksmith's sledge."

Ten years later another volume of American verse was published, not in Massachusetts but in London. It was called "The Tenth Muse lately Sprung up in America," and it contained poems by Mistress Anne Bradstreet. They were written in the conventional and exaggerated manner then in vogue in England, and they reveal on her part no real observation of the new country in which she lived. She seems not to have seen the wide difference between the skies and the trees and the flowers and the birds of New England and those of the old England she had left as a bride. She was born in 1613 and she died in 1672. Among her descendants, alive two hundred years after her own death, were R. H. Dana, the author of "Two Years before the Mast," and Oliver Wendell Holmes, the author of the "Autocrat of the Breakfast Table."

After Mistress Bradstreet the New England writers next to be picked out for mention here are the Mathers. There were many of them, and most of them wrote abundantly. The more noteworthy were Increase Mather, born in 1639 and dying in 1723, and his son, Cotton Mather, born in 1663 and dying in 1728. The son wrote unceasingly and he was well equipped for authorship by deep learning. His own library was by far the largest of any then in private hands in America. It was said that "no native of his country had read so much and retained more of what he read."

Yet he was vain personally and his judgment was capricious. He was one of the most active in the persecution of the alleged witches of Salem in 1692. Three years before the trials of these unfortunate creatures he had published a volume on "Memorable Providences relating to Witchcrafts." Later in life he wrote his most useful book, "Essays to do Good," published in 1710. This was the volume which fell into Franklin's hands when he was a boy and gave him such a turn of thinking as had an abiding influence on his conduct through life.

Cotton Mather

The most of the writing done in New England in the seventeenth century had to do with religion, and so it was also in the early part of the eighteenth century. It was only as the Revolution began to loom up on the horizon that the interests of the church became less exciting than the interests of the state, and politics succeeded religion as the chief topic of the publications of the day.

The growth of the colonies in population and in resources was to give them the strength finally to break the bonds which united them to the British crown. Schools and colleges were established and newspapers were started, until at last there was no one of the little cities along the coast that had not its printing press. A spirit of independence was beginning to develop. In the early years of the eighteenth century there were Americans who thought for themselves and who wrote out boldly what they thought.

It was at the very beginning of the eighteenth century that the two men were born who are beyond all question the two greatest American authors coming to maturity before the revolution. These two men were Jonathan Edwards and Benjamin Franklin. They were products of

the American soil and they grew up under American conditions. They were the first native Americans able to
make a reputation on the other side of the Atlantic and to
hold their own in debate with the best men of Europe.
Of the two, Edwards was three years the older, and for
that reason he may be considered here before Franklin.
It is not to be questioned that Franklin is the more
important of the two because of his services to the country as a whole and because he has left us one book, at
least, which is still read, his delightful "Autobiography."

Jonathan Edwards was born in 1703 in Connecticut.
When only twelve years old he entered Yale College,
being graduated before he was seventeen. He studied
for the ministry and was ordained.
While a student at Yale, and afterward when a tutor in the college,
he paid attention to natural science,
having the same wholesome curiosity
that characterized Franklin. He even
planned a book on this subject, and
gatheied many notes, the result of
his own observations and experiments.
He studied electricity, having ideas
about it long in advance of his time,
and almost anticipating Franklin's

Jonathan Edwards

discoveries. He also turned his acute and searching mind
towards astronomy. But theology was at all times his
chief study, and it is by his writings on religious subjects
that he made his mark in the world.

He was settled as minister of a parish at the age of
twenty-four, being then married. He brought up his
family amid many privations. His health was poor but
his spirit was always strong. He spent thirteen hours a

day in his study.   Even when he rode or walked he kept on thinking; and when from home he had a habit of pinning bits of paper to his clothes, one for every thought he wished to write down on his return, and he would sometimes get back with so many of these scraps that they fluttered all about him.

His great work on the "Freedom of the Will" was published in 1754.  It is now but little read, for we no longer see the subject from Edwards's point of view. But it remains a monument of intellectual effort.   To this day it is probably the most direct and subtle treatise on a philosophical theme written by any American.   It justifies the assertion of more than one European critic that no work of the eighteenth century surpasses it in the vigor of its logic or in the sharpness of its argument. Jonathan Edwards died in 1758, a few days after he had been made president of Princeton College.

QUESTIONS. — What kind of men were the earliest English settlers in America ?   What did they put down in writing ?

Give some account of the most interesting writer among the early adventurers to America.

Describe two examples of early colonial verse — one religious, the other secular.

What was Cotton Mather's connection with the Salem witchcraft trials ?

What changes took place in the general spirit of American literature about the middle of the eighteenth century?

Give an account of the first native American writer who made a reputation in Europe.

NOTE. — There are brief biographies of Capt. John Smith by Mr. C. D. Warner (H. Holt & Co., $1), of Jonathan Edwards, by Prof. A. V. G. Allen (Houghton, Mifflin & Co., $1.25), and of Cotton Mather by Prof. Barrett Wendell (Dodd, Mead & Co., $1).  See also the chapters on this period in the histories of American literature by Prof. C. F. Richardson and Prof. M. C. Tyler.

## III BENJAMIN FRANKLIN

AT the beginning of the eighteenth century, when Queen Anne sat on the throne of Great Britain, there were ten British colonies strung along the Atlantic coast of North America. These colonies were various in origin and ill-disposed one to another. They were young, feeble, and jealous; their total population was less than four hundred thousand. In the colony of Massachusetts, and in the town of Boston, on January 17, 1706, was born Benjamin Franklin, who 'died in the state of Pennsylvania, and in the city of Philadelphia, on April 17, 1790.

In the eighty-four years of his life, Benjamin Franklin saw the ten colonies increase to thirteen; he saw them come together for defense against the common enemy; he saw them throw off their allegiance to the British crown; he saw them form themselves into these United States; he saw the population increase to nearly four millions; he saw the beginning of the movement across the Alleghanies which was to give us the boundless West and all our possibilities 'of expansion. And in the bringing about of this growth, this union, this independence, this development, the share of Benjamin Franklin was greater than the share of any other man.

With Washington, Franklin divided the honor of being the American who had most fame abroad and most veneration at home. He was the only man (so one of his biographers reminds us) who signed the Declaration of Independence, the Treaty of Alliance with France, the Treaty of Peace with England, and the Constitution under which we still live. But not only had he helped to make the nation — he had done more than any one else to form the individual. If the typical American is shrewd, industrious, and thrifty, it is due in a measure to the counsel and to the example of Benjamin Franklin. In "Poor Richard's Almanack" he summed up wisely, and he set forth sharply, the rules of conduct on which Americans have trained themselves now for a century and a half. Upon his countrymen the influence of Franklin's preaching and of his practice was wide, deep, and abiding. He was the first great American — for Washington was twenty-six years younger.

Benjamin was the youngest son of Josiah Franklin, who had come to America in 1682. His mother was a daughter of Peter Folger, one of the earliest colonists. His father was a soap boiler and tallow chandler ; and as a boy of ten Benjamin was employed in cutting wick for the candles, filling the dipping molds, tending shop, and going on errands. He did not like the trade, and wanted to be a sailor. So his father used to take him to walk about Boston among the joiners, bricklayers, turners, and other mechanics, that the boy might discover his inclination for some trade on land.

Franklin tells us that from a child he was fond of reading, and laid out on books all the little money that came into his hands. Among the books he read as a boy were the "Pilgrim's Progress" and Mather's "Essays to do Good"; and this last gave him such a

Franklin's Birthplace

turn of thinking that it influenced his conduct through life and made him always "set a greater value on the character of a *doer of good* than on any other kind of reputation."

It was this bookish inclination which determined his father to make a printer of him, and at the age of twelve he was apprenticed to his brother James. There was then but one newspaper in America — the *Boston News-Letter*, issued once a week. A second journal, the *Boston Gazette*, was started in 1719. At first James Franklin was its printer, but when it passed into other hands he began a paper of his own — the *New England Courant*, more lively than the earlier journals, and more enterprising.  As Benjamin set up the type for his brother's paper, it struck him that perhaps he could write as well as some of the contributors.  He was then a boy of sixteen, and already had he been training himself as a writer.  He had studied Locke "On the Human Understanding," Xenophon's "Memorabilia (Memorable Things) of Socrates," and a volume of the "Spectator" of Addison and Steele.  This last he chose as his model, mastering its methods, taking apart the essays to see how they were put together, and so finding out the secret of its simple style, its easy wit, its homely humor.  His first attempts at composition were put in at night under the door of the printing house; they were approved and printed; and after a while he declared their authorship.

For a mild joke on the government James Franklin was forbidden to publish the *New England Courant*, so he canceled his brother's apprenticeship and made over the paper to Benjamin.  But the indentures were secretly renewed, and the elder brother treated the younger with increasing harshness, giving him an aversion to arbitrary power which stuck to him through life.

At length the boy could bear it no longer, and he left his brother's shop.  James was able to prevent him from getting work elsewhere in Boston, so Benjamin slipped off on a sloop to New York.  Failing of employment there, he went on to Philadelphia, being then seventeen.  He arrived there with only a "Dutch dollar" in his pocket.  Weary and hungry, he asked at a baker's for a three-penny-worth of bread, and, to his surprise, he received three great puffy rolls.  He walked off with a roll under each arm and eating the third; and he passed the house of a Mr. Read, whose daughter stood at the door, thinking the young stranger made a most awkward, ridiculous appearance, and little surmising that she was one day to be his wife.

Franklin worked at his trade in Philadelphia for nearly two years. In 1724 he crossed the ocean for the first time to buy type and a press, but was disappointed of a letter of credit Governor Keith had promised him. He found employment as a printer in London, and he came near starting a swimming school; but in 1726, after two years' absence, he returned to Philadelphia, and there he made his home for the rest of his life. He soon set up for himself as a printer, and, as he was more skillful than his rivals and more industrious, he prospered, getting the government printing and buying the *Pennsylvania Gazette*.

He married Deborah Read; and he made many friends, the closest of whom he formed into a club called the "Junto," devoted to inquiry and debate. At his suggestion the members of this club kept their books in common at the clubroom for a while; and out of this grew the first circulating library in America — the germ of the American public library system. And in 1732 he issued the first number of "Poor Richard's Almanack," which continued to appear every year for a quarter of a century.

It was "Poor Richard's Almanack" which first made Franklin famous, and it was out of the mouth of Poor Richard that Franklin spoke most effectively to his fellow-countrymen. He had noticed that the almanac was often the only book in many houses, and he therefore "filled all the little spaces that occurred between the remarkable days in the calendar with proverbial sentences, chiefly such as inculcated industry and frugality as the means of procuring wealth, and thereby securing virtue; it being

# Poor RICHARD improved:

BEING AN

# ALMANACK

AND

# *EPHEMERIS*

OF THE

MOTIONS of the SUN and MOON;

THE TRUE

PLACES and ASPECTS of the PLANETS;

THE

*RISING* and *SETTING* of the *SUN*;

AND THE

Rifing, Setting *and* Southing *of the* Moon;

FOR THE

YEAR of our LORD 1758:

Being the Second after LEAP-YEAR.

Containing alfo,

The Lunations, Conjunctions, Eclipfes, Judgment of the Weather, Rifing and Setting of the Planets, Length of Days and Nights, Fairs, Courts, Roads, &c. Together with ufeful Tables, chronological Obfervations, and entertaining Remarks.

Fitted to the Latitude of Forty Degrees, and a Meridian of near five Hours Weft from *London* ; but may, without fenfible Error, ferve all the NORTHERN COLONIES.

By *RICHARD SAUNDERS*, Philom.

*PHILADELPHIA*

Printed and Sold by B. FRANKLIN, and D. HALL.

## August hath xxxi Days.

| | D. | H. |
|---|---|---|
| New ☽ | 3 | 8 aft. |
| First Q. | 11 | 11 aft. |
| Full ● | 18 | 8 aft. |
| Last Q. | 25 | at noon. |

☊ { 1 ♋ 25 Deg. / 11 24 / 21 24 }

Planets Places.

| D. | ☉ | ♄ | ♃ | ♂ | ♀ | ☿ | ☽ L. |
|---|---|---|---|---|---|---|---|
| | ♌ | ♓ | ♐ | ♎ | ♋ | ♌ | |
| 1 | 9 | 2 | 10 | 4 | 0 | 13 | S. 1 |
| 6 | 14 | 2 | 10 | 7 | 6 | 23 | N. 4 |
| 12 | 19 | 2 | 10 | 10 | 13 | ♍ 4 | 4 |
| 17 | 24 | 1 | 10 | 14 | 19 | 13 | S. 1 |
| 22 | 29 | 1 | 11 | 17 | 25 | 21 | 5 |
| 27 | ♍ 24 | 1 | 11 | 20 | ♌ 1 | 28 | . 1 |

| D. | ☽ rise | ☽ sou. | T. | |
|---|---|---|---|---|
| 1 | 2 27 | 10 12 | 12 | 21 |
| 2 | Moon | 11 2 | 1 | 22 |
| 3 | sets. | 11 51 | 2 | 23 |
| 4 | A. | 12 37 | 3 | 24 |
| 5 | 8 17 | 1 23 | 3 | 25 |
| 6 | 8 47 | 2 7 | 4 | 26 |
| 7 | 9 15 | 2 51 | 5 | 27 |
| 8 | 9 40 | 3 32 | 6 | 28 |
| 9 | 10 8 | 4 14 | 6 | 29 |
| 10 | 10 33 | 4 57 | 7 | 30 |
| 11 | 11 5 | 5 40 | 8 | 31 |
| 12 | 11 41 | 6 26 | 8 | Aug. |
| 13 | Morn | 7 17 | 9 | |
| 14 | 12 15 | 8 10 | 10 | 3 |
| 15 | 1 3 | 9 8 | 11 | 4 |
| 16 | 2 2 | 10 6 | 12 | 5 |
| 17 | Moon | 11 7 | 1 | 6 |
| 18 | rises | Morn | 1 | 7 |
| 19 | A. | 12 8 | 2 | 8 |
| 20 | 8 10 | 1 7 | 3 | 9 |
| 21 | 8 46 | 2 6 | 4 | 10 |
| 22 | 9 19 | 3 0 | 5 | 11 |
| 23 | 9 53 | 3 49 | 6 | 12 |
| 24 | 10 33 | 4 42 | 7 | 13 |
| 25 | 11 14 | 5 34 | 8 | 14 |
| 26 | 11 54 | 6 25 | 8 | 15 |
| 27 | Morn | 7 15 | 9 | 16 |
| 28 | 12 28 | 8 8 | 10 | 17 |
| 29 | 1 27 | 9 0 | 11 | 18 |
| 30 | 2 18 | 9 49 | 12 | 19 |
| 31 | 3 19 | 10 37 | 1 | 20 |

*Richard* says, *'Tis foolish to lay out Money in a Purchase of Repentance*; and yet this Folly is practised every Day at Vendues, for want of minding the Almanack. *Wise Men*, as *Poor Dick* says, *learn by others Harms, Fools scarcely by their own*; but, *Felix quem faciunt aliena Pericula cautum.* Many a one, for the Sake of Finery on the Back, have gone with a hungry Belly, and half starved their Families; *Silks and Sattins, Scarlet and Velvets*, as *Poor Richard* says, *put out the Kitchen Fire.* These are not the *Necessaries* of Life; they can scarcely be called the *Conveniencies*, and yet only because they look pretty, how many *want* to *have* them. The *artificial* Wants of Mankind thus become more numerous than the *natural*; and, as *Poor Dick* says, *For one* poor *Person, there are an hundred* indigent. By these, and other Extravagancies, the Genteel are reduced to Poverty, and forced to borrow of those whom they formerly despised, but who through *Industry* and *Frugality* have maintained their Standing; in which Case it appears plainly, that a *Ploughman on his Legs is higher than a Gentleman on his Knees*, as *Poor Richard* says. Perhaps they have had a small Estate left them,

D which

more difficult for a man in want to act always honestly, as, to use here one of these proverbs, 'It is hard for an empty sack to stand upright.'" By these pithy, pregnant sayings, carrying their moral home, fit to be pondered in the long winter evenings, Franklin taught Americans to be thrifty, to be forehanded, and to look for help from themselves only.

The rest of the almanac was also interesting, especially the playful prefaces; for Franklin was the first of American humorists, and to this day he has not been surpassed in his own line. The best of the proverbs — not original, all of them, but all sent forth freshened and sharpened by Franklin's shrewd wit — he "assembled and formed into a connected discourse, prefixed to the almanac of 1757, as the harangue of a wise old man to the people attending an auction."

Thus compacted, the scattered counsels sped up and down the Atlantic coast, being copied into all the newspapers. The wise "Speech of Father Abraham" also traveled across the ocean and was reprinted in England as a broadside to be stuck up in houses for daily guidance; it was twice translated into French — being probably the first essay by an American author which had a circulation outside the domains of our language. It has been issued since in German, Spanish, Italian, Russian, Dutch, Portuguese, Gaelic, and Greek. Without question it is what it has been called — "the most famous piece of literature the colonies produced."

No man had ever preached a doctrine which more skillfully showed how to get the best for yourself; and no man ever showed himself more ready than Franklin to do things for others. He invented an open stove to give more heat with less wood, but he refused to take out a

patent for it, glad of an opportunity to serve his neighbors ; and this invention of Franklin's was the beginning
of the great American stove trade of to-day.  He founded
the first fire company in Philadelphia, and so made a
beginning for the present fire departments.  He procured
the reorganization of the night watch and the payment of
the watchmen, thus preparing for the regular police force
now established.  He started a Philosophical Society ; and
he took the lead in setting on foot an academy — which
still survives as the University of Pennsylvania.

While he was doing things for others, others did things
for him, and he was made Clerk of the General Assembly
in 1736, and Postmaster of Philadelphia in 1737.  In 1750
he was elected a member of the Assembly, and in 1753
he was made Postmaster-general for all the colonies.  In
1748 he had retired from business, having so fitted his
practice to his preaching that he had gained a competency
when but forty-two years old.

The leisure thus acquired he used in the study of
electrical science, then in its infancy.  He soon mastered
all that was known, and then he made new experiments
with his wonted ingenuity.  He was the first to declare
the identity of electricity and lightning.  Using a wet
string, he flew a kite against a thunder cloud, and drew a
spark from a key at the end of a cord.  The lightning rod
was his invention.  Of his investigations and experiments
he wrote reports that were printed in England and translated in France.  The Royal Society voted him a medal ;
the French king had the experiments repeated before him ;
and both Harvard and Yale made Franklin a Master of
Arts.

But Franklin was not long allowed to live in philosophic
retirement. · When the French War broke out he was

appointed one of the commissioners sent by Pennsylvania to a congress of the colonies held at Albany. He wrote a pamphlet which aided the enlisting of troops ; and by pledging his own credit he helped General Braddock to get the wagons needed for the unfortunate expedition against Fort Duquesne. He drew up a Plan of Union on which the colonies might act together, and thus anticipated the Continental Congress of twenty years later.

In 1757, when Pennsylvania could no longer bear the interference of the governor appointed by the proprietors, Franklin was sent to London as the representative of his fellow-citizens. It was more than thirty years since he had left England, a journeyman printer ; and now he returned to it, a man of fifty, the foremost citizen of Philadelphia, the author of " Father Abraham's Speech," and the discoverer of many new facts about electricity.

He was gone nearly five years, successfully pleading the cause of Pennsylvania, and publishing a pamphlet which helped to prevent the restoration of Canada to the French. Then he came home, to be met by an escort of five hundred horsemen, and to be honored by a vote of thanks from the Assembly.

But the dispute with the proprietors of the colony blazing forth again, Franklin was sent back to London once more to oppose the Stamp Act. He returned to England in 1764, at first as agent of Pennsylvania only, but in time as the representative of New Jersey, Georgia, and Massachusetts also ; and he remained for more than ten years, pleading the cause of the colonists against the king, and explaining to all who chose to listen the real state of feeling in America. He did what he could to get the first Stamp Act repealed. He gave a good account of himself when he was examined by a committee of the House of Commons. He wrote telling papers of all sorts: one a set of " Rules for Reducing a Great Empire to a Small One," and another purporting to advance the claim of the King of Prussia to levy taxes in Great Britain just as the King of England asserted the right to lay taxes on the Americans. He lingered in London, doing all he could to avert the war which he felt to be inevitable. At last, in 1775, less than a month before the battle of Lexington, he sailed for home.

On the day after he landed he was chosen a member of the Second Continental Congress. He acted as Postmaster-general. He signed the Declaration of Independence, making answer to Harrison's appeal for unanimity : " Yes, we must all hang together, or assuredly we shall all hang separately." Then there appeared to be a hope that France might be induced to help us ; and in September, 1776, Franklin was elected envoy. Being then seventy years old, he went to Europe for the fourth time.

In France he received such a welcome as no other American has ever met with. He was known as an author, as a philosopher, as a statesman. The king and the queen, the court and the people, all were his friends. His portraits were everywhere, and his sayings were repeated by everybody. In the magnificence of the palace of Versailles Franklin kept his dignified simplicity ; and with his customary sagacity he turned to the advantage of his country all the good will shown to himself. After Burgoyne's surrender the French agreed to an open alliance with the United States, and Franklin, with his fellow-commissioners, signed the treaty in 1778.

During the war Franklin remained in France as American Minister, borrowing money, forwarding supplies, exchanging prisoners, and carrying on an immense business on behalf of his country. As one of his biographers remarks, Franklin "stood in the relation of a navy department" to John Paul Jones when that hardy sailor was harassing the British coasts in the "Bonhomme Richard," — as his vessel was named, after "Poor Richard." He bore the brunt of the countless difficulties which beset the American representatives in Europe. At last Cornwallis surrendered; and, with Adams and Jay, Franklin signed the treaty of peace with Great Britain, in September, 1783. The next year Jefferson went to France, and in 1785 relieved Franklin, who was allowed to return to America, being then seventy-nine years of age.

His "Autobiography," which he had begun in 1771 in England, and had taken up again in France in 1783, he hoped to be able to finish now that he was at home again and relieved from the responsibility of office. But he was at once elected a councillor of Philadelphia, and although he would have liked the leisure he had so hardly earned, he felt that he had no right to refuse this duty. Then was the "critical period of American history," and Franklin was kept busy writing to his friends in Europe encouraging and hopeful accounts of our affairs.

When the constitutional convention met, Franklin was made a member "that, in the possible absence of General Washington, there might be some one whom all could agree in calling to the chair." After the final draft of the Constitution was prepared, Franklin made a speech pleading for harmony, and urging that the document be sent before the people with the unanimous approbation of the members of the convention. Then, while the last members were signing, he said that he had seen a sun painted on the back of the President's chair, and during the long debates when there seemed little hope of an agreement he had been in doubt whether it was taken at the moment of sunrise or sunset ; "but," he said, "now at length I have the happiness to know that it is a rising and not a setting sun."

He was now a very old man. He said himself : "I seem to have intruded myself into the company of posterity, when I ought to have been abed and asleep." His cheerfulness never failed him, and although he suffered much, he bore up bravely. "When I consider," he wrote in 1788, "how many more terrible maladies the human body is liable to, I think myself well off that I have only three incurable ones : the gout, the stone, and old age." He looked forward to death without fear, writing to a friend that, as he had seen "a good deal of this world," he felt "a growing curiosity to be acquainted with some other."

For a year or more before his death he was forced to keep his bed. When at last the end was near and a pain seized him in the chest, it was suggested that he change his position and so breathe more easily. "A dying man can do nothing easily," he answered; and these were his last words. He died April 17, 1790, respected abroad and beloved at home.

In many ways Franklin was the most remarkable man who came to maturity while these United States were yet British colonies ; and nothing, perhaps, was more remarkable about him than the fact that he was never "colonial" in his attitude. He stood before kings with no uneasy self-consciousness or self-assertion ; and he faced a committee of the House of Commons with the calm strength of one thrice armed in a just cause. He never bragged or blustered ; he never vaunted his country or himself. He was always firm and dignified, shrewd and good-humored.

Philad. Nov. 20. 1780

Dear Friend,

I hope soon to be in a situation when I can contribute largely and fully to my Friends in France, without the perpetual Interruption I now daily meet with. At present I can only tell you that I am well

And thus esteem you,
And t'Abbé Morellet,
And M. Cabbanis,
And love dear Madame
Helvetius,   infinitely.

Adieu,

Your most affectionately

B Franklin

a I receiv'd several Productions
of the Academy at Auteuil
which gave me great Pleasure.

Humor, indeed, he had so abundantly that it was almost a failing. Like Abraham Lincoln, another typical American, he never shrank from a jest. Like Lincoln, he knew the world well and accepted it for what it was, and made the best of it, expecting no more. But Franklin lacked the spirituality, the faith in the ideal, which was at the core of Lincoln's character. And here was Franklin's limitation : what lay outside of the bounds of common sense he did not see — probably he did not greatly care to see ; but common sense he had in a most uncommon degree.

One of his chief characteristics was curiosity — in the wholesome meaning of that abused word. He never rested till he knew the why and the wherefore of all that aroused his attention. As the range of his interests was extraordinarily wide, the range of his information came to be very extended also. He was thorough, too ; he had no tolerance for superficiality ; he went to the bottom of whatever he undertook to investigate. He had the true scientific spirit. He loved knowledge for its own sake, although he loved it best, no doubt, when it could be made immediately useful to his fellow-men. In science, in politics, in literature, he was eminently practical ; in whatever department of human endeavor he was engaged, he brought the same qualities to bear. For the medal which was presented to Franklin in France the great statesman Turgot composed the line :

Eripuit cœlo fulmen sceptrumque tyrannis[1];

and it was true that Franklin had faced the ministers of George III. with the same fearless eye that had gazed at the thunder cloud.

[1] He has seized the lightning from heaven and the scepter from tyrants.

There is an admirable series in course of publication containing the lives of American men of letters, and there is an equally admirable series containing the lives of American statesmen. In each of these collections there is a volume devoted to Benjamin Franklin; and if there were also a series of American scientific men, the story of Franklin's life would need to be told anew for that also. No other American could make good his claim to be included even in two of these three collections.

As science advances, the work of the discoverers of the past, even though it be the foundation of a new departure, may sink more and more out of sight. As time goes on, and we prosper, the memory of our indebtedness to each of the statesmen who assured the stability of our institutions may fade away. But the writer of a book which the people have taken to heart is safe in their remembrance; and, perhaps, to-day it is as the author of his "Autobiography" that Franklin is best known. If he were alive, probably nothing would surprise him more than that he should be ranked as a man of letters, for he was not an author by profession. He was not moved to composition by desire of fortune or of fame; he wrote always to help a cause, to attain a purpose; and the cause having been won, the purpose having been achieved, he thought no more about what he had written. He had a perfect understanding of the people he meant to reach, and of the means whereby he could best reach them.

Most of these writings were mere journalism, to be forgotten when its day's work was done; but some of them had so much merit of their own that they have survived the temporary debate which called them into being. Wit is a great antiseptic, and it has kept sweet the "Whistle," the "Petition of the Left Hand," the "Dialogue between

Franklin and the Gout," and the lively little essay on the
"Ephemera." Wisdom is not so common even now that
men can afford to forget "Father Abraham's Speech," the
"Necessary Hints to Those that would be Rich," and
"Digging for Hidden Treasure." Much of his fun is as
fresh and as unforced now as it was a century and a half
ago. Much of the counsel he gives so pleasantly, so
gently, so wisely, is as needful now as it was when "Poor
Richard" sent forth his first almanac.

He taught his fellow-countrymen to be masters of the
frugal virtues. He taught them to attain to self-support
that they might be capable of self-sacrifice. He taught
them not to look to the government for help, but to stand
ready always to help the government if need be. There
are limits to his doctrine, no doubt ; and there are things
undreamt of in Franklin's philosophy. Yet, his philosophy
was good so far as it went; in its own field to this day
there is no better. Common sense cannot comprehend
all things ; but it led Franklin to try to help people to be
happy, for he believed that this was the best way to make
them good.

It was by watching and by thinking that Franklin
arrived at his wisdom ; and it was not by chance that he
was able to set forth his views so persuasively. Skill in
letters is never a lucky accident. How rigorously he
trained himself in composition he has told us in the
"Autobiography"—how he pondered on his parts of
speech and practiced himself in all sorts of literary gym-
nastics. And of the success of his training there is no
better proof than the "Autobiography" itself. It is a
marvelous volume, holding its own to-day beside "Robinson Crusoe," as one of the books which are a perpetual
delight to young and to old. to the scholar familiar with

Franklin's achievements, and to the boy just able to spell out its simplest sentences. It is one of the best books of its kind in any language, and it abides as the chief monument of Benjamin Franklin's fame.

QUESTIONS. — Tell the story of Franklin's life in Boston.

Describe the publication that first made Franklin famous.

Mention several facts which go to show that Franklin preached self-ishness in order that he might encourage philanthropy. How did he spend his leisure ?

Trace Franklin's public career before the war for independence.

Speak of his public services during the war.

What things happened to prevent Franklin from completing, during the critical period of American history, a literary work upon which he had long been engaged ?

Describe Franklin's last years.

Show how Franklin's chief characteristic was manifested in his life.

In what three fields was Franklin famous?

How was Franklin able to invest his writings with the qualities that have preserved them from sharing the neglect usually bestowed upon productions of their class?

NOTE. — There is an edition of Franklin's complete works, including his correspondence (G. P. Putnam's Sons, out of print). The fullest edition of the "Autobiography" is that of Mr. John Bigelow (J. B. Lippincott & Co., 3 vols., $4.50). There is a condensed edition in the Riverside Literature series (Houghton, Mifflin & Co., 40 cents) ; and the same series has also one number containing "Poor Richard's Almanack" and other selections from Franklin's writings (15 cents).

There are biographies by James Parton (Houghton, Mifflin & Co., 2 vols., $5), by J. T. Morse, Jr. (American Statesmen series, Houghton, Mifflin & Co., $1.50), and by Prof. J. B. McMaster (American Men of Letters series, Houghton, Mifflin & Co., $1 25).

## IV  WASHINGTON IRVING

THE first American man of letters, Benjamin Franklin, was a man of letters only incidentally, and, as it were, accidentally; for he was a printer by trade, a politician by choice, and never an author by profession.

The first American who frankly adopted literature as a calling, and who successfully relied on his pen for his support, was Washington Irving. The first American who was a professed author was not Franklin, who was born a Bostonian and who died a Philadelphian ; but Irving, who was born, who lived, and who died a New Yorker.

Washington Irving's father was a Scotchman who had settled in New York a dozen years before the Revolution. During the British occupation of Manhattan Island, the Irvings were stanch patriots, and did what they could to relieve the sufferings of the American prisoners in the city. A few months before the evacuation day, which the inhabitants of New York were to keep as a holiday for a century after, Washington Irving was born, on April 3, 1783, being, like Benjamin Franklin, the youngest of many sons. The boy was not baptized until after Washington and his army had entered the city. "Washington's work is ended," said the mother, "and the child shall be named after him."

New York came out of the Revolution half in ruins, and wasted by its long captivity; its straggling streets filled only the toe of the island, and it had less than twenty-five thousand inhabitants. But the little city began to grow again as soon as peace returned. It was in New York, in 1789, that Washington took the oath as the first President of these United States. One day not long thereafter a Scotch maidservant of the Irvings, struck with the enthusiasm which everywhere greeted the great man, followed him into a shop with the youngest son of the family, and said, "Please, your honor, here's a bairn was named for you." Washington placed his hand on the head of the boy, and gave him his blessing.

New York was then the capital of the country; it was a spreading seaport; it retained many traces of its Dutch origin; it had in its streets men of every calling and of every color. Here the boy grew up happy, going to school and getting knowledge out of books, but also lingering along the pier heads, and picking up the information to be gathered in that best of universities — a great city.

He was playful rather than studious ; and although two of
his brothers had been educated at Columbia College, he
neglected to enter — a blunder which he regretted all his
life, and which Columbia regrets to this day.  Perhaps
the fault may be charged to his poor health, for the sake
of improving which he began to live much in the open
air, making voyages up the Hudson in sloops that then
plied as packets between New York and Albany.  The
first sail through the Highlands was to him a time of
intense delight, and the Catskill Mountains had the most
witching effect on his boyish imagination.  Nowadays we
are used to hearing the Hudson praised, but it was Irving
who first proclaimed its enchanting beauty ; and it was
when he was a dreaming youth that he discovered its
charm.

Much against the grain he began to read law, but his
studies were only fitful.  One of his brothers established
a daily paper in 1802 ; and to this Washington, then only
nineteen, contributed a series of occasional essays under
the signature of Jonathan Oldstyle.  These were humorous and sportive papers, and they were copied far and
wide, as the sayings of Poor Richard had been quoted
fifty years before.

The next summer, Irving made a journey up the
Mohawk, to Ogdensburg, and thence to Montreal.  The
year after, being then just twenty-one, his brothers sent
him to Europe in the hope that the long sea voyage and
the change of scene might restore him to health.  Irving
had to be helped up the side of the ship, and the captain
said to himself, "There's a chap who will go overboard
before we get across."  The voyage did him good, and
from Bordeaux he went to Genoa ; he pushed on as far
as Sicily, and came back to Rome ; then turned north to

Paris, and finally crossed over to London. After a year and a half of most enjoyable wandering he took ship again for home, and arrived safely in New York after a stormy passage of sixty-four days.

Washington Irving now returned to the study of law, and he was soon admitted to the bar — a proof rather of the mercy of the examiners than of the amount of his legal knowledge. He never made any serious attempt to earn his living as a lawyer. Only a few weeks after his admission, he, his brother William, and his friend James K. Paulding, sent forth the first number of "Salmagundi," an irregular periodical suggested, perhaps, by the "Spectator" of Addison and Steele, but droller, more waggish, and with sharper shafts for folly as it flies. The first number was published in January, 1807, and caused not only great amusement, but also much wonder as to the real names of the daring authors. The twentieth, and final number, appeared a year later. Irving always spoke of it as a very juvenile production, and such it is, no doubt; but it was brisk and lively, indeed it was brighter than anything of the ·kind yet written in America; and in the papers contributed by Washington Irving we can see the germs of certain of his later works.

One of these papers pretended to be a chapter from "The Chronicles of the Renowned and Ancient City of Gotham," [1] and Irving's next literary undertaking was a burlesque history of New York, which he and his brother Peter undertook to write together. The brothers had heaped up many notes when Peter was called away, and Washington, changing the plan of the book, began to write it alone. He started on his labor joyful and happy,

---

[1] Gotham was an English village proverbial for the blundering simplicity ·' of its inhabitants. Irving humorously applied the name to New York.

but he ended it in the depths of sorrow.   He was in love
with Miss Matilda Hoffman, a charming and graceful girl,
and their marriage had been agreed on.   Suddenly, having
caught a bad cold, which went to her lungs, after a brief
illness she died.   Irving, then twenty-six, bore the blow
like a man, but he carried the scar to the grave.   To his
most intimate friends he never mentioned her name.   For
several months after her death he wandered aimlessly,
unable to apply himself to anything.   Then he went back
to his work, and finished the burlesque history of New
York.   It may seem strange that a book of such bubbling
humor should be the result of those days of darkness ; but
as has often happened in literature, the writings at which
people laugh longest are the work of men who are grave
rather than gay.

" A History of New York, by Diedrich Knickerbocker,"
was published in December, 1809.   It was a playful parody
of the annals of New Amsterdam, laughing at the Dutch
burghers who had founded the capital of New Netherlands,
and making fun of their manners and their customs.   In the
method of the author there was more than a trace of the
manner of "Don Quixote," and its irony was as gentle and
as good-natured.   That " Knickerbocker " was received with
acclamation there is no wonder.   It was the most readable
book which had yet appeared in America — for Franklin's
" Autobiography " did not get into print until 1817.   At
home it gave a name to a time in New York's history and
to a set of the city's traditions, a name even now in popular
use, for every one knows what is meant when we speak of
a person or a thing as a " Knickerbocker."   Abroad it
revealed to the critics that American life was to have its
own literature.   Scott read the book aloud to his family.
The book still delights all who can appreciate its delicate

fun; nowadays our taste in humor is more highly spiced than it was when "Knickerbocker" appeared, but it is not purer.

The protests which a few descendants of the Dutch founders of the city ventured to put forth were laughed aside, for the public had taken the joke and were unwilling to have the fun spoiled. Yet it is to be regretted that, in his youth, Irving should have echoed the British scoffs at the Dutch. We are rarely fair to our rivals, and the Dutch had not only taught the British agriculture and commerce, but they had swept the British Channel with a broom at their admiral's masthead; and so the British disliked them. Foremost in art, and in law, and in education, the Dutch had exerted a most wholesome influence on American institutions — the chief of which, our common-school system, was probably derived from Holland. Irving did not think of this when he made fun of the Dutchmen of New Amsterdam, or he did not know it. There was no malice in his satire; but thoughtlessness sometimes hurts as severely.

For ten years after the publication of "Knickerbocker," Irving brought forth no new work. He lingered and loitered and hesitated. He went to Washington for a season, and he edited a magazine in Philadelphia. When the War of 1812 broke out, he was stanchly patriotic, although he deplored the war itself. After the wanton destruction of the capitol at Washington by the British, he offered his services to the governor of New York, and was appointed aid and military secretary. In 1815, after peace was proclaimed, he made another voyage across the Atlantic to England to see his brother. Intending only a brief visit, he was absent from home, as it happened, for seventeen years.

From rough notes in a common place book

By the author of the Sketch Book

46

Paris April 25th 1821 — made a compact with
a friend this morning to [call?] Talma the
great French tragedian. He has a suite of
apartments in a hotel in the rue [de?] [Helder?]
[conjuring?] but is about to build a [house?]

In England and in Scotland he met the literary celebri-
ties of the day, among them Sir Walter Scott. At last he
turned again to literature, and the first number of " The
Sketch Book of Geoffrey Crayon, Gent." was published in
New York in 1819. The " Sketch Book" was a miscellany
of essays, sketches, and tales. As Irving wrote to a friend,
he had "attempted no lofty theme, nor sought to look wise
and learned." "I have preferred," he said, "addressing
myself to the feeling and fancy of the reader more than to
his judgment." The first number contained the "Voyage
to England" and "Rip Van Winkle." Its success was
instant and remarkable. As the following numbers appeared, they began to be reprinted in British periodicals ;
and so Irving, still detained in England, gathered the first
four numbers into a volume and issued it in London. The
series extended to seven numbers in America ; and later on
both sides of the Atlantic the complete book was published
in two volumes toward the end of 1820. Thereafter Irving
had a secure place in the history of English literature.

The charm of the "Sketch Book" is not difficult to
define. Sunshine lights up every page, and a cheerful
kindliness glows upon them all. From the "Sketch
Book" we must date the revival of Christmas feasting,
although, no doubt, Irving was aided powerfully by Dick-
ens, who took the American as his model in more ways
than we are wont to remark. It is the "Sketch Book"
which has sent thousands of Americans across the Atlantic, passionate pilgrims to Stratford, entranced wanderers
through Westminster Abbey, and happy loiterers in the
country churchyards of England. Although in the second
number of the "Sketch Book," Irving warned "English
Writers on America" that their malicious reports were
certain to cause ill will — as, indeed, they have done — no

American ever felt more kindly toward England ; and when he died, Thackeray, calling him "the first ambassador whom the New World of Letters sent to the Old," praised him for his constant good will to the mother country.

Though Irving was stalwart in his Americanism always, — he refused, for example, to write for the *Quarterly Review*, because it had ever been a bitter enemy to America — he had a sincere liking for England, and a hearty appreciation of its picturesque possibilities. This was shown to advantage in his next book, "Bracebridge Hall," published in 1822 ; and it was seen even in the book that followed this — the "Tales of a Traveler," published in 1824. These two collections may be described not unfairly as continuations of the "Sketch Book," the former containing chiefly essays and sketches, and the latter, only short stories and character portraits. There is in all the libraries of England no book more filled with the gentle spirit of English country life than "Bracebridge Hall"; and Irving himself never wrote a more delicately humorous sketch than the "Stout Gentleman," in that volume.

In the history of the short story, one of the most useful as it is one of the most popular of literary forms, Irving holds a high place. The "Sketch Book" owed much of its success to "Rip Van Winkle" and the "Legend of Sleepy Hollow" — tales of a kind till then unknown in English literature ; and "Dolph Heyliger," in "Bracebridge Hall," is a worthy third, while "Wolfert Webber," in the "Tales of a Traveler," is not far behind. Considering their strength, Irving's short stories have a singular simplicity ; they are slight in plot and simple in the character drawing. He understood his own powers clearly. "I consider a story merely as a frame on which to stretch my materials," so he wrote to a friend ; "it is the play of thought, and sentiment, and language; the weaving in of characters, lightly yet expressively delineated; the familiar and faithful exhibition of scenes of common life; and the half-concealed vein of humor that is often playing through the whole; these are among what I aim at."

This is a fair statement of the qualities which give charm to "Rip Van Winkle" and its fellows. Little did Irving foresee that these tales of his were but the first fruits of that abundant harvest, rich in local flavor, which later American story tellers were to raise, each on his own half-acre. Hawthorne and Poe, Bret Harte and Cable, are all followers in Irving's footsteps.

It was while Byron and Scott were the leaders of English letters that Irving published the "Sketch Book," and made good his own title to an honorable position in literature. By the publication of "Bracebridge Hall," and of the "Tales of a Traveler," his footing became firmer, no doubt; but he did not advance further. Irving was in Spain in 1826, and there he remained for more than three years — the most laborious and fruitful years of his life. He had gone to Spain to translate some important Spanish documents concerning Columbus; but getting interested in the character and in the career of Columbus, he soon settled down to the preparation of a biography of his own. He took his task seriously; he spared no pains in getting every date right and every proper name exact; he rewrote as often as he discovered new material. He knew that a biography was not a work of fiction, to be warped at the will of the writer, but rather a monument to be built slowly out of actual facts.

When the "Life of Columbus" appeared in 1828, it was seen at once that Irving had not only the gift of the born story teller, but also the sterner virtues of the historian.

To this day, despite the storm of dispute which has raged over every item of Columbus's career, Irving's biography remains a valuable authority. A most devoted student of the details of Columbus's life has declared that Irving's "is a history written with judgment and impartiality, which leaves far behind it all descriptions of the discovery of the New World published before or since." If to-day it were edited with notes embodying the latest information, it would hold its own against all newcomers. The reader sees a completed painting, and not the raw materials out of which he is invited to make a picture for himself.

The "Life of Columbus" was soon followed by a book about the "Companions of Columbus," and by the "Chronicle of the Conquest of Granada," which Irving regarded as his best work, and which Coleridge greeted as a masterpiece of its kind. Just what its kind is, it is not easy to declare, but perhaps it may be described as a record of fact presented with the freedom the author had used in writing fiction. In the main, it is a true story, but it is as obedient to the hands of the story teller as though he had made it up. The narrative is spirited, the style is delightful, and there is a never-ending play of sentiment and humor.

These are the qualities which grace yet another Spanish book, the "Alhambra," perhaps the most fascinating of all Irving's writings. The "Alhambra" is a medley of travel, sketches, character studies, and brief tales ; it is what Prescott called it : a Spanish "Sketch Book." The method of the author is the same as in his "Sketch Book," only he has changed the model who poses before him. "Brace-bridge Hall" is not more English than the "Alhambra" is Spanish. It is full of the sights and the sounds of Spain ; and there it is pleasant to gaze upon this reflection of Moorish architecture and Iberian landscape and Spanish character in the clear mirror held up to nature by the genial New Yorker.

The "Alhambra" was published in 1832, and after an absence of seventeen years, Irving returned to his native city. He found New York wonderfully expanded ; in the scant half-century of his life, the twenty thousand population had increased to two hundred thousand. He was made heartily welcome, and his fellow-citizens promptly bestowed on him the compliment of a public dinner. From that day to his death he was the acknowledged head of American letters. He bore his honors as easily as he bore all things.

He made a home for himself in the village of Tarrytown, New York, on the banks of the Hudson he loved, and near the Sleepy Hollow he had celebrated. Here, in the stone cottage of Sunnyside, he settled down, enjoying the leisure which now and again he varied by periods of hard labor. He made a tour on the prairies ; he wrote an account of the settlement of Astoria in Oregon ; he put into shape the travels of Captain Bonneville ; and he began work on a history of the conquest of Mexico, but with his wonted generosity he surrendered the subject to Prescott when he was told that the younger author was about to undertake it.

Thus ten years passed away ; and in 1842 Irving was making ready to write the life of Washington, when he was surprised by the appointment of Minister to Spain. Daniel Webster was then Secretary of State, and he knew no American could be more welcome in Spain than the biographer of Columbus. A foreign appointment is almost the only honor a republic can bestow upon its foremost authors ; the first of American men of letters, Benjamin Franklin, had been Minister to France ; and after Irving, similar positions were to be held by Motley, and Bancroft, and

Lowell.   Irving accepted the appointment, and spent four years in Madrid, with occasional visits to Paris and to London.   Then in 1846 he came home again, and settled down at Sunnyside for the last thirteen years of his happy life.

Among the labors of these later years were the extending of an earlier and briefer biography of Goldsmith, an account of Mahomet and his contemporaries, and a vol-

Sunnyside

ume of miscellanies, called "Wolfert's Roost," containing sketches and stories like those in the "Sketch Book" and the "Alhambra."   Tarrytown is only a few miles from New York, and Irving was a frequent visitor to the city of his birth.   He has been described as walking along Broadway with his head "slightly inclined to one side, the face . . . smoothly shaven," and the eyes "twinkling" with kindly humor and shrewdness.   There was a chirping, cheery, old-school air in his whole appearance.

Washington Irving was at that time perhaps the best
known of living Americans ; and he was then engaged on
the biography of the best known of all Americans alive or
dead. The first volume of Irving's "Life of Washington"
appeared in 1855, and the work was completed in 1859.
Irving was doubtful about its reception, but it became
instantly popular; it had a very large sale, and it was
lauded by his fellow-historians. Bancroft praised the style,
calling it "masterly, clear, easy." Prescott wrote : "You
have done with Washington just as I thought you would,
and, instead of a cold marble statue of a demigod, you
have made him a being of flesh and blood, like ourselves
— one with whom we can have sympathy."

In the year in which the final volume of the "Washington" was published, Irving died at Sunnyside on November
28, 1859, being then seventy-six years old. American men
of letters are a long-lived race ; Franklin, Emerson, Bryant,
and Whittier lived to be older than Irving, while Longfellow and Lowell were only a little younger at their
deaths. Like Irving, they all died full of years and full of
honors ; they all had led happy lives.

No later American writer has surpassed him in charm.
Before Irving had discovered the beauty of the Hudson,
the river was as lovely as it is to-day, but its legends were
little known. He it was who peopled the green nooks of
Sleepy Hollow and the rocky crags of the Catskills. His
genius was not stalwart or rugged, and it did not conquer
admiration ; it won its way softly, by the aid of sentiment and of humor. "Knickerbocker's History," and the
"Sketch Book," and the "Alhambra," are his titles to
fame ; not the "Columbus" or the "Washington." He
had the conscience of the historian and he could color his
narrative artistically and give it movement; but others

could do this as well as he. But to call into being a civilization, to give to a legend the substance of truth, to present a fiction, so that it passes for fact and is accepted by the people and gets into common speech — this is a feat very few authors have ever accomplished. Irving did it, and his greatest work is not any one of his books — it is the Knickerbocker legend.

QUESTIONS. — What events were happening in and around New York during the early years of Irving's life?

What can you say about " Salmagundi "?

Describe Irving's first important literary work.

How was Irving occupied during the ten years that followed the publication of " Knickerbocker "?

What was Thackeray's characterization of Irving?

Discuss Irving's place in the history of the short story.

Comment upon four books which grew out of Irving's third visit to Europe.

How were the ten years of Irving's life passed after his return home?

Describe his last great literary work.

What was the nature of Irving's genius?

NOTE. — The authorized edition of Irving's works is published by G. P. Putnam's Sons (12 vols., $15). Selections from the " Sketch Book " are published by the American Book Company (20 cents) and in two numbers of the Riverside Literature series (Houghton, Mifflin & Co., 15 cents each). The whole " Sketch Book " and the " Tales of a Traveler," annotated by Dr. W. L. Phelps, and the " Alhambra," annotated by Mr. Arthur Marvin, are in the Student's series (G. P. Putnam's Sons, $1). An annotated edition of the " Tales of a Traveler " is issued by the American Book Company (50 cents). Another edition by Prof. Brander Matthews and Prof. G. R. Carpenter is published by Longmans, Green & Co. ($1).

There are biographies by Pierre M. Irving (G. P. Putnam's Sons, 3 vols., $4.50) and by Mr. C. D. Warner in the American Men of Letters series (Houghton, Mifflin & Co., $1.25).

For criticism, see Lowell's " Fable for Critics "; Thackeray's " Nil Nisi Bonum " (in " Roundabout Papers "); Mr. Warner's " Work of Washington Irving " (in Harper's Black and White series ); Mr. W. D. Howells (in " My Literary Passions "); G. W. Curtis (in " Literary and Social Addresses "); and Prof. C. F. Richardson (in his history of " American Literature ").

## V  JAMES FENIMORE COOPER

As Irving was the first American author whose writings won favor outside of his native land, so another New Yorker, James Fenimore Cooper, was the first American author whose works gained a wide circulation outside of his native tongue. While the "Sketch Book" was as popular in Great Britain as in the United States, the "Spy," and the "Pilot," and the "Last of the Mohicans," were as popular on the continent of Europe as they were in America, North and South. To the French and the Germans, to the Italians and the Spaniards, James Feni-

more Cooper is as well known as Walter Scott.  Irving was
the first American writer of short stories, but Cooper was
the first American novelist ; and, to the present day, he
is the one American novelist whose fame is solidly established among foreigners.

Born at Burlington, New Jersey, on September 15, 1789,
Cooper was taken in infancy to Otsego Lake in the interior

Otsego Hall

of New York ; and here, at the point where the Susque-
hanna streams forth on its way to join the distant Chesapeake, Cooper's father built the stately mansion called
Otsego Hall.  The elder Cooper was the owner of many
thousand acres along the head waters of the Susque-
hanna, and in this wilderness, centering around the
freshly founded village of Cooperstown, the son grew into
boyhood.  He could pass his days on the beautiful lake,

shut in by the untouched forest, or in the woods themselves which rose with the hills and fell away into the
valleys.  He slept at night amid the solemn silence of a
little settlement, a hundred miles beyond the advancing
line of civilization.

Hard as it may be for us now to realize it, a century ago
"the backwoods" were in the state of New York.  It was
only during the Revolution that the people of our stock
made ready to push their way across the Alleghanies.  For
years after the nineteenth century had begun, the only
white men who sped down the Mississippi, or toiled slowly
up against its broad current, spoke another tongue than
ours.  Although Cooper lived in New York, it was in the
backwoods that he spent his childhood, and to Cooperstown
he returned at intervals throughout his life.  Backwoods
scenes and backwoods characters he could always recall
at will from his earliest recollections.  The craft of the
woodsman, the tricks of the trapper, all the delicate art of
the forest, were familiar to Cooper from his youth up, just
as the eery legends of North Britain and stirring ballads
of the Border had been absorbed by Walter Scott.

Franklin never had the chance of a college education;
Irving was fitted for Columbia, but did not enter; Cooper
entered Yale, but did not graduate — and the fault was his
own.  It was thought that the sea would cure his tendency
to frolic.  The Naval Academy had not then been established, and the customary training for a career on a man-
of-war was to gain experience in the merchant marine.
So in the fall of 1806, when Cooper was seventeen, he
sailed on a merchant vessel for a year's cruise, shipping
before the mast, and seeing not a little hard service.
Soon after his return he received a commission as a mid-
shipman in the regular navy.

It was a time of peace, although the war with Great Britain already was foreseen. In 1808 Cooper was one of a party sent to Oswego, on Lake Ontario, to build a six-teen-gun brig. In 1809 he was left for a while in com-mand of the gunboats on Lake Champlain. In the same year he was attached to the " Wasp," then commanded by Lawrence — the Lawrence who was soon to command the "Chesapeake" in the action with the "Shannon," and who was to die with the immortal phrase on his lips, "Don't give up the ship!" Although Cooper saw no fighting during the three years and a half in which he wore the uniform of his country, he greatly increased his store of experience, adding to his knowledge of life before the mast on a merchant vessel an understanding of life on the quarter-deck of a man-of-war, besides gaining acquaint-ance with the Great Lakes.

In January, 1811, Cooper married a Miss De Lancey, with whom he was to live happily for more than forty years. Apparently at the request of his bride, he resigned from the navy in May. He dwelt at Mamaroneck in West-chester county, New York, for several years, at first with his wife's father, and then in a hired house. In 1817, after a three years' stay in Cooperstown, he went back to Westchester, the home of his wife's childhood, and there he remained for five years. Seemingly content with the simple life of a well-to-do country gentleman, Cooper reached the age of thirty without any attempt at author-ship — without even the hankering after pen and ink which is the characteristic of most predestined authors. The novelist flowers late ; Scott was forty-three when his first novel, "Waverley" was published ; and Hawthorne was forty-six when the "Scarlet Letter" appeared ; but they had been writing from their boyhood.

Cooper's entry into authorship was almost accidental. Reading some cheap British novel, he was seized with the idea that he could do as well himself; and the result was his first book, "Precaution," published late in 1820. "Precaution" was an imitation of the average British novel of that time; it had merit equal to that of most of its models; it was a tale of life in England, and there was nothing to show that its author was not an Englishman. Indeed, when the book was republished in London, it was reviewed with no suspicion of its American authorship.

That Cooper, a most loyal and ardent American, should write a second-hand story of this sort, shows how complete was the colonial dependence of the United States on Great Britain in the first quarter of the nineteenth century — so far at least as letters were concerned. American literature did not exist. No one had yet declared that the one thing out of which an American literature could be made was American life. When Cooper's "Precaution" was written, Irving's "Sketch Book" was being published in parts; it was still incomplete, and half of the sketches in the book were from English subjects.

Yet it seems to have struck Cooper that if he did not fail with a novel describing British life, of which he knew little, he might succeed with a novel describing American life, of which he knew much. "Waverley" had been published in 1814, and in the next six years had appeared eight others of the "Scotch novels," as they were called; and in the very year of Cooper's first book, Scott had crossed the Border and produced in "Ivanhoe" really the first English historical novel, applying the method of the anonymous Scotch stories to an English theme. Cooper perceived that the same method could be applied to an American historical theme; and in the "Spy," which

Dear Sir

I shall be in Town the latter part of this week in the beginning of the next and will call on you immediately. I have endeavoured these four several times since your return to Town to see you but have not been able to find you at home. I write this to let you know that I have not forgotten your new schedule and as written before but thought I should be able to go to Town before this —

Yours &c —

Francis Cochran

Liverpool - Feb. 9 - 1820

L. Bracke &c —

was published in 1821, he gave us the first American historical novel.

The "Spy" is a story of the Revolution, and its scene is laid in the Westchester which Cooper knew so well, and which had been a neutral ground, harried in turn by the British and the Americans : the "Cowboys" and the "Skinners." The time and the place were well chosen, and they almost sufficed of themselves to lend romance to any adventures the author might describe; and even better chosen was the central figure, 'Harvey Birch,' one of the most interesting and effective of romantic characters. To the Spy himself, mysterious but winning, was chiefly due the instant success — and the success of the story was extraordinary, not only in the United States at first, and a few months later in Great Britain, but on the continent of Europe. It was translated into French by the translator of the Waverley novels; and it was afterward translated into most of the modern languages in turn.

Encouraged by the plaudits of the public on both sides of the Atlantic, Cooper wrote another story, the "Pioneers," published in 1823. As the "Spy" was the first American historical novel, so was the "Pioneers" the first attempt to put into fiction what is perhaps as worthy of record as anything in American history — the life on the frontier and the character of the backwoodsman. Here Cooper was on firm ground; and although he did not fully realize the opportunity before him, his book was a revelation to the rest of the world. In it appeared for the first time one of the very greatest characters in fiction, the old woodsman, Natty Bumppo — the Leatherstocking who was to give his name to the series of tales which to-day is Cooper's best monument. In this first book we have but a faint sketch of the character the author afterward worked

out with loving care. Rarely is there a successful sequel
to a successful novel, but Cooper returned to Leatherstocking again and again, until the history of his adventures
was complete in five independent tales, the composition of
which extended over eighteen years.

Leaving for the moment Cooper's other writings, it may
be well to note here that the "Pioneers" was followed in
1826 and 1827 by the "Last of the Mohicans" and the
"Prairie," and in 1840 and 1841 by the "Pathfinder" and
the "Deerslayer." This was the order in which they were
written, but very different is the order in which they are
to be read when we wish to follow the career of Natty
Bumppo from the days of his youth, and to trace the development of his noble and captivating character. The
latest written is the earliest to be read in the sequence of
events ; after the "Deerslayer" comes the "Last of the
Mohicans," followed by the "Pathfinder" and then the
"Pioneers," until in the "Prairie" the series ends with
the death of Leatherstocking. The five tales vary in value,
no doubt, but taken altogether they reveal a marvelous gift
of narration, and an extraordinary fullness of invention.
Merely as stories their interest is unfailing, while they are
ennobled by the character of Natty.

Even before the publication of the "Pioneers," in which
he introduced the American Indian into fiction, Cooper
planned another story which was as daring a novelty. In
1821, the author of the Waverley novels, then unascer-
tained, published the "Pirate." In Cooper's presence,
the argument was advanced that Scott could not be the
unknown author, since he was a lawyer, and this story
revealed a knowledge of the ocean such as no landsman
could have. Cooper, who had followed the sea himself,
maintained that the "Pirate" showed that its author was

not a sailor, since far greater effects could have been got out of the same materials if the writer had been a seafarer by profession. To prove his point, Cooper determined to write a sea story. Sailors there had been in fiction before, but no novel the scene of which was laid on the ocean; and Cooper's friends tried to convince him that the public at large could not be interested in a life so technical as the seaman's.

But Cooper persevered, and in 1823 he published the "Pilot," the first salt-water novel ever written, and to this day one of the very best. Its nameless and mysterious hero was a marine Harvey Birch; obviously he had been modeled upon the Paul Jones whose name is held in terror to this day on the British coasts he harassed. In Long Tom Coffin, the Nantucket whaler, Cooper created the only one of his other characters worthy to take place beside Leatherstocking; and Tom, like Natty, is simple, homely, and strong. In writing the "Pilot," Cooper evidently had in mind the friends who thought it impossible to interest the general reader in a tale of the ocean, and he laid some of his scenes on land; but it is these very passages which are tedious to-day, while the scenes at sea keep their freshness and have still unfailing interest.

In his second sea tale, the "Red Rover," published in 1829, Cooper avoided this blunder; after the story is fairly started the action passes continuously on the water, and the interest is therefore unbroken. The "Red Rover" may be said to be wholly a tale of the ocean, as the "Last of the Mohicans" is wholly a tale of the forest. Whether he was on the green billows or under the green trees, Cooper was completely at home; he drew from his own experience; he told what he had seen, what he knew. He wrote ten sea tales in all, of which the "Two Admirals" and "Wing-and-Wing," both published in 1842, are the best after the "Pilot" and the "Red Rover." In 1839 he sent forth his "History of the United States Navy," to this day the only authority for the period of which it treats.

It is by the "Spy," by the five "Leatherstocking Tales," and by the four or five foremost of the "Sea Tales" that Cooper's fame must be maintained. But he wrote many other novels, most of them of little importance. Some of them, like the "Wept of Wish-ton-wish," were American in subject; and some were European, like the "Bravo" and the "Headsman." These last were the result of a long visit Cooper paid to Europe, extending from 1826 to 1833. In Paris he had the pleasure of meeting Scott; and in Paris also he had the pleasure of defending his country against ignorant insults.

There is no need now to deny that Cooper seems to have enjoyed a dispute, and that he never went out of his way to avoid a quarrel. After he returned to the United States he became involved in numberless arguments of all sorts, personal, journalistic, literary, historical. He was frank, opinionated, and absolutely certain that he always had right on his side. Sure of his ground, he bore himself bravely and battled stanchly to repel any attacks he had invited.

His private life was most fortunate. His home was happy, and his wife and children were devoted to him. He had many friends; and his best friends were the best citizens of New York. When he moved to that city, in 1822, he founded a club, called sometimes after him, but more generally the "Bread and Cheese Lunch." To this club belonged Chancellor Kent; the poets Fitz-Greene Halleck and William Cullen Bryant; S. F. B. Morse, the inventor of the telegraph; and other representatives of the arts, the sciences, and the learned professions. Before Cooper went to Europe in 1826 these friends gave him a public dinner, at which Chancellor Kent presided and at which De Witt Clinton, the governor of the State, Winfield Scott, the head of the army, and Charles King, the future president of Columbia College, were present. After his return from Europe in 1833, the same group of distinguished men tendered to him another banquet, which he declined.

Nearly a score of years after, when he was sixty years old, and when he had lived through the storm of abuse which he had injudiciously aroused, his friends again made ready to give him a public testimonial of their regard; but before the arrangements were perfected he died. He had retired to Cooperstown years before, and there with his family he had been happy, superintending work on his farm, and writing when he chose. His death took place on September 14, 1851, at Cooperstown, to which he had been taken as an infant three score years before. Had he lived another day, he would have completed his sixty-second year. His wife outlived him less than five months.

A few days after his death a meeting of prominent men was held, over which Washington Irving presided, and as a result of this, William Cullen Bryant was asked to deliver a discourse on the life and writings of Cooper. This oration, spoken early in the next year, remained the best account of the novelist until the admirable biography in the American Men of Letters series appeared in 1882.

A consideration of Cooper's place in English literature involves a comparison with Scott. In the first place, the Scotchman was the earlier of the two; it was he who widened the field of the romance; it was he who pushed the novel to the front and made fiction the successful rival of poetry and the drama; it was he who showed all men how an historical novel might be written. Cooper is the foremost of Scott's followers, no doubt, and in skill of narration, in the story-telling faculty, in the gift of imparting interest to the incidents of a tale, Cooper at his best is not inferior to Scott at his best. But Scott had far more humor and far more insight into human nature.

Like Scott, Cooper was a writer of romance; that is to say, he was an optimist, an idealizer — one who seeks to see only the best, and who refuses to see what is bad. Scott chose to present only the bright side of chivalry, and to make the Middle Ages far pleasanter than they could have been in reality. Probably Scott knew that the picture he gave of England under Richard the Lion-Hearted was misleading; certainly he knew that he was not telling the whole truth. Cooper's red Indians are quite as real as Scott's black knights, to say the least. Cooper's Indians are true to life, absolutely true to life — so far as they go. Cooper told the truth about them — but he did not tell the whole truth. He put forward the exception as the type, sometimes; and he always suppressed some of the red man's ugliest traits. Cooper tells us that the Indian is cruel as Scott tells us that a tournament was often fatal; but he does not convey to us any realization of the ingrained barbarity and cruelty which was perhaps the chief characteristic of the Indian warrior. This side of the red man is kept in the shadow, while his bravery, his manliness, his skill, his many noble qualities, are dwelt on at length.

Time may be trusted safely to make a final selection from any author's works, however voluminous they may be, or however unequal. Cooper died almost exactly in the

# 68 AMERICAN LITERATURE

middle of the nineteenth century; and already it is the
"Spy" and the "Leatherstocking Tales" and four or five
of the "Sea Tales" which survive, because they deserve to
survive, because they were at once new and true when they
were written, because they remain to-day the best of their
kind. Cooper's men of the sea, and his men of the forest
and the plain, are alive now, though other fashions in fiction have come and gone. Other novelists have a more
finished art nowadays, but no one of them all succeeds
more completely in doing what he tried to do than did
Cooper at his best. And he did a great service to American literature by showing how fit for fiction were the
scenes, the characters, and the history of his native land.

QUESTIONS. — Describe the conditions existing in western New
York at the birth of the first American novelist.

Tell the story of Cooper's early life and training on land and on sea.
What changes in his way of living followed upon his marriage?

What circumstances attending upon Cooper's entrance upon a literary career show the dependent position of American literature?

Describe the first American historical novel.

Describe the series of fictions of which Natty Bumppo is the hero.

Declare the circumstances under which the first sea tale was written.

Compare Cooper's relations with the general public with his associations in private life.

Compare Cooper with Scott.

What were Cooper's great services to literature?

NOTE. — There are many editions of Cooper's stories. The best is that containing introductions by his daughter (Houghton, Mifflin & Co., 32 vols., $1 a vol.).

The only biography is that of Prof. T. R. Lounsbury in the American Men of
Letters series (Houghton, Mifflin & Co., $1.25).

For criticism, see Bryant's Oration (in his "Essays, Tales, and Orations");
Lowell's "Fable for Critics"; Thackeray's "On a Peal of Bells" (in "Roundabout
Papers"); and Prof. C. F. Richardson (in his history of "American Literature").

For a discussion of "Colonialism in the United States," see Mr. H. C. Lodge's
"Studies in History."

## VI  WILLIAM CULLEN BRYANT

WASHINGTON IRVING and James Fenimore Cooper were New Yorkers both by descent and by residence, but William Cullen Bryant, who lived at the same time, though a New Yorker by residence, was of the purest New England descent.   Like Benjamin Franklin, the forerunner of Irving and Cooper, Bryant left the town of his birth to become the foremost citizen of a great city.   He was born in the village of Cummington, in western Massachusetts, November 3, 1794, so he was eleven years younger than Irving and five years younger than Cooper.   He survived

Irving nearly twenty years, and died in New York in 1878. When he first saw the light, the United States were only fifteen in number, and Washington, the first President, was still at the head of the little nation. He lived to see the celebration of the hundred years of our independence, and the admission of the thirty-eighth state.

That he should have lived to the age of eighty-three is the more remarkable, as he had a feeble frame and no great stock of strength. As a young child he was " puny and very delicate in body, and of a delicate nervous organization." From the beginning he was forced to save himself in every way, and to order his life regularly, denying himself many things which others used freely. To the last year of his life he was regular in his habits, rising betimes, eating little, exercising much, and going to bed early. From his earliest youth he had himself under almost perfect control. In his life, as in his poetry, his simplicity was almost severe.

His father was a country doctor, and also represented his native town in the Massachusetts legislature. His mother was descended from John Alden and his wife Priscilla, whose courtship has been told in verse by Longfellow, another of their descendants. Bryant was ready for college very young, learning Latin from Vergil's "Æneid" and Greek from the Greek Testament. He began to make verses very early, and when scarce ten years old, so one of his biographers tells us, he "received a ninepenny coin from his grandfather for a rimed version of the first chapter of the book of Job." Even when he was but a little boy he wished to be a poet. He knew by heart the rude verses of Watts's hymns and the finished couplets of the English poet Pope. It was from Pope that he learned the art of verse ; and Pope was no bad teacher, for he was an artist in rime and rhythm.

In the fall of 1810, Bryant, then not quite sixteen, entered the sophomore class at Williams College. At the end of the collegiate year he asked for and received an honorable dismissal from Williams, intending to enter the junior class at Yale. But his father could not afford to support him at New Haven, and to his lasting regret the poet was deprived of the profit of a full college course. He spent the summer at home, working on the farm, and reading

Bryant's Home, Cummington, Mass.

diligently the books of his father's library, medical and poetical. A few days before January 1, 1812, he began the study of law; and to law his attention was given for more than ten years. He did not like the law, and he gave it up at the first opportunity; but while it was his calling he did his work loyally and thoroughly.

The *North American Review* was founded in 1815 by a little group of Bostonians, of whom Richard Henry Dana was one; it was a magazine like the British reviews of the time. To this review certain of Bryant's poems were sent; and when one of these was read aloud at a meeting of the editors, Dana smiled and said, "You have been imposed upon. No one on this side of the Atlantic is capable of writing such verse."

When they had assured themselves that they had not been imposed upon, the editors published two of the poems in the *North American Review* for September, 1817. One was called "Thanatopsis," and it had been composed six years before, when the poet was not yet eighteen. It was, as a critic has well said, "not only the finest poem which had been produced on this continent, but one of the most remarkable poems ever produced at such an early age." Since its original appearance in print, the author has revised it and improved it; but from the first it was seen to be among the foremost moral poems of our language. Though the poet might afterward equal it, he could never surpass it. In the same number of the *Review* appeared also his verses now known as "An Inscription for the Entrance to a Wood." In 1818 the *Review* published Bryant's "Lines to a Waterfowl." Thereafter there was no doubt that the English language had gained a new poet.

Dr. Bryant died in 1820, and a year later the poet, being then twenty-six years of age, married Miss Fairchild. In 1822 Bryant was invited to deliver the Phi Beta Kappa poem at Harvard, and he wrote the "Ages," which pleased its hearers so much that the poet yielded to their requests, and gathered his scattered verses into a little volume — a thin book, but containing that which is destined to a long life in literature.

This earlier poetry of Bryant's has for us a double interest, that due to its own merit, which is undoubted, and that due to its influence upon other native poets in opening their eyes to the life about them. In this last quarter of the nineteenth century it is very hard for us to understand how completely American authors depended upon Great Britain in the first quarter of the century. Not only was everything judged by British standards — everything was seen through British spectacles.

Bryant was the first American who discovered that the flowers and the birds of New England were not those of old England. He took this discovery to heart, and acted upon it always; and every later American poet has followed his example. After Bryant's first volume of poems appeared, the nightingale became as silent in American verse as it had always been in American woods. Bryant was the earliest of our American authors to tell in poetry the facts of our own natural history. He always kept close watch on nature: when only twelve years old, he wrote verses about the eclipse of 1806. "Thanatopsis" is imbued with a spirit of loving tenderness toward nature. The "Yellow Violet," written in 1814, is probably the first poem devoted to an actual American flower ; and it reveals anew the poet's ability to see for himself what no poet had noted before, as in the final line of this stanza, for example : —

> Thy parent sun, who bade thee view
> Pale skies, and chilling moisture sip,
> Has bathed thee in his own bright hue,
> And streaked with jet thy glowing lip.

In 1825 Bryant gave up the law finally, resolved to earn his living by his pen. He removed to New York, where he was to reside for the next half century. He was appointed editor of the *New York Review*, to which he contributed many poems, among them that beginning : —

> The melancholy days are come, the saddest of the year.

To live, that when thy summons comes to join
The innumerable caravan which moves
To that mysterious realm where each shall take
His chamber in the silent halls of Death,
Thou go not; like the quarry-slave at night,
Scourged to his dungeon, but sustained and soothed
By an unfaltering trust, approach thy grave
Like one who wraps the drapery of his couch
About him and lies down to pleasant dreams.

          William Cullen Bryant

One of the poems by other authors which he published in the pages of the *New York Review* was the "Marco Bozzaris" of Fitz-Greene Halleck. But the *Review* did not prosper. Before it died Bryant had become an editorial writer on the *Evening Post*. After the *New York Review* ceased to be published, Bryant joined two friends in editing an annual, called the *Talisman*, which made three appearances only. In 1829 the editor in chief of the *Evening Post* died, and Bryant was promoted to his place. He already owned one eighth of the paper, and he was now enabled to increase his holding to one half. This share he retained to his death, and it became increasingly profitable as the years went by. For the last half of his long life Bryant had an assured income from property in his own control. He had to work hard, but he was his own master.

Bryant gave up law for journalism at a time when there was still an old-fashioned primness among literary people : it was a time when the law was commonly personified as "Themis," when authors were called the "literati," when writing verses was termed "toying with the Muses," and when there were not a few other affectations. But it was a time when American authors were beginning to write prose which is still read with pleasure. There was a pleasanter and more artistic atmosphere in New York, where many authors resided, than in any other American city. New York, already marked as the business metropolis of the country, was also the literary center of the Union when Bryant moved to it. And by the authors and artists of New York Bryant was made welcome. He lectured before the newly organized National Academy of Design, and he became a member of the Cooper Club, better known as the "Bread and Cheese Lunch."

Although American literature had thus begun, it was still in its infancy. The reading public was very small, and the magazines were few and struggling. One could hardly earn a living as a man of letters; to support a family by literature was impossible. Irving was a bachelor, and Cooper had means of his own. Besides, literature at best is better as a staff than it is as a crutch. There is no doubt, therefore, that Bryant did well in relying on journalism for his bread, although he might hope now and again to pay for his butter by literature. Both the editor and the author earns his living by his pen, yet there is little or no other likeness between them. The author says once for all what he has to say, and he says it as best he can ; while the journalist, if he says anything once, must repeat it again and again, since that is his chief method of producing his effect. Then, again, the author tries to find subjects of eternal interest, ever fresh and never stale ; while the journalist is condemned to the perpetual discussion of timely topics of present importance. Perhaps it is not too much to suggest that the habit of journalism tends to unfit a man for literature.

In journalism, as in authorship, character tells for as much as ability ; and upon the newspaper he conducted Bryant imposed his own lofty ideals. He had definite political principles, and these he applied and advocated, however much their unpopularity might impair the profits of his paper. He held fast to his principles, even when they forced him to leave the political party with which he had hitherto been acting. It was his belief, for example, that the interference of government in the affairs of the citizen did more harm than good ; and it is upon this question of more or less governmental control of private business that the people of the United States have divided into parties in the past and will divide again in the future. Like Franklin, Bryant preached the doctrine of self help.

But although as a journalist Bryant took high ground and defended it firmly, he was never carried away by the fury of partisan discussion. In his editorial writings, as in his poetry, the tone is full of dignity. Calm in his strength, he was both temperate in expressing his opinions and good-tempered. He fought fairly and he respected his adversary. He was never a snarling critic either of men or of measures. He elevated the level of the American newspaper, but it was by his practice, not by his preaching. He was choice in his own use of words, and there was in the office of the *Evening Post* a list of words and phrases not allowed in its pages. But he was not a stickler for trifles, and he had no fondness for petty pedantries.

The editorial articles which Bryant wrote for his paper day by day for more than fifty years have never been collected, and of course they never will be, though they are a history of the United States during the half-century which no student of the times can afford to neglect. The letters written to the *Evening Post*, when he was on his travels, have most of them been reprinted. He made a tour on the prairies in 1832, and in 1834 he went to Europe to stay a year and a half, spending his time in France, Italy, and Germany. In 1845 he crossed the ocean a second time, and paid his first visit to England. In later years he went to Europe four times more, once going on to Egypt and the Holy Land. He also visited Cuba and Mexico. In 1850 he gathered the best of the letters he had sent to the *Evening Post* from abroad and published them in a volume, as the "Letters of a Traveler"; and in 1869 he made a second collection called "Letters from the East." The interest of these two books is due rather to their author than to their own merits, although these are not slight; anything Bryant wrote had a value of its own; but he lacked the ease, the lightness, the familiarity which are to be found in the letters of the ideal traveler. He was a poet; and his best work was in verse, not in prose.

And yet his newspaper letters, and a few tales in the *Talisman*, and a few criticisms in the early Reviews, do not make up the total of his prose works. Bryant was also a public speaker. Upon a score of solemn occasions the poet was the orator of the day; and these addresses are preserved in a volume of the collected edition of his works. At the death of Cooper, Bryant was invited to deliver a memorial oration, in which he paid to his departed friend the full measure of laudation, not overpraising, but carefully valuing, and setting the fame of the novelist upon firm foundations. At the death of Irving, and of Halleck, Bryant was again called upon, and he again responded with speeches worthy not only of the subject but also of himself.

More than once he was the speaker on great civic occasions when the citizens of New York needed a mouthpiece. Yet he was not a born orator; he lacked the physical strength, the sweep of gesture, the persuasive voice, the contagious enthusiasm, the kindling fire, which make up the gift of eloquence. His addresses were always written out carefully; they were always prepared with a full appreciation of the demands of the occasion, and with a full understanding of his own limitations; they were always stately and impressive, yet were never stiff or labored.

The fame of the orator, and of the traveler, and of the journalist, perishes swiftly, while that of the poet endures. Bryant did not allow his duty to his newspaper wholly to absorb his time. To poetry he was devoted his whole life long, although the body of his verse is not great. In 1831 he published a volume of his poetry containing four score more poems than had appeared in the collection of ten years before. He sent a copy of this to Irving, who procured its republication in London, and who, in deference to British readers, softened the line which declares that

> The British soldier trembles
> When Marion's name is told.

More than thirty years later, in 1863, Bryant published what may be called the second volume of his poetry, to which he gave the simple title of "Thirty Poems." Among these later poems were the defiant refrain of "Not Yet," and the resolute stanzas, "Our Country's Call," written in the dark days at the outbreak of the Rebellion and nobly eulogized in Lowell's "On Board the Seventy-Six." His later verses were added in successive editions of his complete poems.

In the course of his travels and of his studies he had made himself familiar with French and German, Spanish and Italian, while he had deepened his knowledge of Greek and Latin. He was fond of translating from the modern poets of other lands, and in this delicate art he was fairly successful, although he lacked the sure touch of Longfellow. In the fall of 1863 he translated the fifth book of the "Odyssey." Encouraged by the way in which it was received, he turned to the "Iliad" and began to translate passages of that.

In the summer of 1866 his wife died, and the poet felt her loss keenly; it unfitted him for severe work, and yet made it advisable that he should keep occupied. He again turned to Homer, and in 1870 he published his complete translation of the "Iliad," following it two years later with a version of the "Odyssey." Bryant was successful in giving the impression of ease and of elevation, and his version of Homer has generally been accepted as one of the best of the many recent metrical translations.

Bryant had long passed three score years and ten when he finished his task of turning the great Greek poem into English verse. He was hale in his old age, exercising regularly, eating sparingly, taking great care of himself, and retaining full possession of his powers. At the age of eighty-four he delivered an address in Central Park at the unveiling of the bust of Mazzini, the Italian patriot. The day was hot, and he spoke with slight shelter from the sun. After the ceremony he walked across the Park to a friend's house, but as he mounted the steps he fell back suddenly. He was taken to his own home, where he lingered for a fortnight, dying June 12, 1878.

Bryant's place in the history of American literature is easy to declare: he was a pioneer and leader. He was the earliest poet of nature as it is here in the United States, seeing it freshly for himself and not repeating at second hand what British poets had been saying about nature as it is in the British Isles. The love he bore to nature was almost a passion, like the love he had for his country. His verse is stately and reserved, sometimes perilously near to frigidity. Unfailingly elevated as it is, the reader sometimes finds himself longing in vain for a playful stroke or a touch of humor. There is a lack of lightness in Bryant's poetry — perhaps even a lack of ease. Yet there is a lyric swing in the "Song of Marion's Men" and a singing quality to the "Planting of the Apple Tree."

It is not fair to suggest that Bryant's muse always sits lonely on a chill and lofty peak. No doubt there is often an absence of warmth — due perhaps to the constant self-control which had become second nature. Bryant likened George Washington to the frozen Hudson flowing full and mighty beneath its shield of ice ; and one could fairly apply the figure to the poet himself. He, too, had a grand simplicity of style. There is a stern and determined vigor

Bryant's Home, Roslyn, L.I.

in certain of his stanzas that Washington might have enjoyed. Take the famous quatrain from the "Battle-Field," for example, —

> Truth crushed to earth shall rise again :
> The eternal years of God are hers :
> But Error, wounded, writhes in pain
> And dies among his worshipers.

His hatred of shams and gauds kept his verse simple and clear — undefiled by jingling conceits or petty prettinesses ; it is sustained nearly always at the same high level. Although his best poems are not many, he wrote surprisingly little that fell below his average.   It is said that an old young man makes a young old man.   Certainly the saying was true of Bryant as a poet : he was mature very early in life and he kept his freshness to the end. " Thanatopsis " was written when he was young, and the " Flood of Years " when he was old ; and a comparison shows that there has been no growth : the thought is as deep in the first poem as in the second, and the expression is as free and as noble.

QUESTIONS. — Discuss briefly : (1) Bryant's early acquaintance with verse ; (2) his career as a student.

Comment upon Bryant's first four important poems.   What double interest have these poems for us?

What is to be said for and against journalism as a calling for a person of literary tastes?    What was Bryant's ideal in journalism?

What portion of his journalistic writing did he care to preserve?

What is to be said of Bryant as a public speaker?

What is Bryant's place in the history of American literature?

What is one criticism most likely to be made upon Bryant's poetry? And what can be said in answer to this criticism?

NOTE. — The only complete edition of Bryant's works is that published by D. Appleton & Co. (4 vols., $12), who also issue the " Poems " alone (Household edition, 1 vol., $1.50; Cabinet edition, 1 vol., $1).   It is best to beware of unauthorized editions of the poems, which are none of them complete.   " Sella," with " Thanatopsis " and other poems, are included in one number of the Riverside Literature series (Houghton, Mifflin & Co., 15 cents).

There are biographies by Mr. Parke Godwin (D. Appleton & Co., 2 vols., $6), and by Mr. John Bigelow (in American Men of Letters series, Houghton, Mifflin & Co., $1.25).

For criticism, see Lowell's " Fable for Critics "; Alden's " Studies in Bryant"; Prof. C. F. Richardson (in his history of " American Literature "); Mr. E. C. Stedman (in his " American Poets ").

Fitz-Greene Halleck

# VII FITZ-GREENE HALLECK AND JOSEPH RODMAN DRAKE

In the first quarter of the nineteenth century New York grew more rapidly than any other town in the Union, and it soon became the literary center of the United States. There were men of letters also in Philadelphia and in Boston; and reviews and magazines were published in both of these cities; but it was in New York that Irving and Cooper resided, and they were the chiefs of our young literature. Other literators there were also, in the same city,

.of less widespread fame. One of them was Irving's friend and literary partner, James K. Paulding, joint author of "Salmagundi." Another was Clement C. Moore, the writer of the favorite juvenile poem beginning : —

'Twas the night before Christmas, when all through the house,
Not a creature was stirring, not even a mouse.

Men of more force and originality than either Moore or Paulding were the two friends, Fitz-Greene Halleck and Joseph Rodman Drake, who joined forces in 1819 in writing a series of occasional poems, signed "Croaker," or "Croaker & Co.," the authorship of which was for a while as great a puzzle to the inhabitants of New York as that of "Salmagundi" had been ten years earlier. These "Croaker Poems" began to appear in March, 1819, in the *New York Evening Post*, the long-established newspaper of which Bryant was to .become the editor a few years later. They continued to be published in the columns of this journal two or three times a week for two or three months, to the prolonged amusement of all New York.

They made fun of many of the men and women of the day. They bristled with bright jests on the topics of the time ; and this is the reason why they are little read at this late date. Allusions which were very plain to those who lived in the compact little town of New York at the beginning of the nineteenth century are not now easily understood by the widespread inhabitants of the United States at the end of the nineteenth century. Jokes which nobody could fail to see when they were first rimed are not now visible without laborious explanation ; and as a result the "Croaker Poems" are no longer read except by students of history.

Thursday Evening.

My dear Sir,

I have your note —
weather &c willing, I will strive
to be at Stony Creek on Saturday morning at 10 oclock &
hope for the pleasure of passing
the day with you,

most truly yours
F. G. Halleck.

W. B. Elliot Eq

85

But these verses deserved their swiftly won reputation, no doubt. Even to-day it is not hard to see that they were the work of two clever young men who found real enjoyment in the exercise of their cleverness and in the aiming of their swift shafts of satire. Some of the poems were written by Halleck alone and some by Drake alone, and some by both of them together, one suggesting the needed point and the other finding the metrical expression. There is in the best of them a youthful flow of high spirits, which is evidence of the delight the young poets took in their work. It is recorded that on one occasion, "Drake, after writing some stanzas and getting the proof from the printer, laid his cheek down upon the lines he had written, and looking at his fellow poet with beaming eyes, said, 'O, Halleck, isn't this happiness?'"

One of the poems originally published under the signature of "Croaker & Co." has survived because its theme was not temporary, like the themes of its fellows, and because the poet treated the loftier subject he chose with an appropriate breadth and vigor. This poem is the heroic address to the "American Flag," beginning :—

> When Freedom from her mountain height,
>   Unfurled her standard to the air,
> She tore the azure robe of night,
>   And set the stars of glory there!

It was written by Drake, before he reached the age of twenty-four. The final four lines as he originally drafted them were these :—

> And fixed as yonder orb divine,
>   That saw thy bannered blaze unfurled,
> Shall thy proud stars resplendent shine,
>   The guard and glory of the world.

Halleck suggested instead of these lines this quatrain, and Drake willingly accepted his suggestion : —

> Forever float that standard sheet !
>  Where breathes the foe but falls before us ?
> With Freedom's soil beneath our feet,
>  And Freedom's banner streaming o'er us !

Young as he was when he wrote the stirring stanzas of this patriotic appeal, Drake was already the author of the

Joseph Rodman Drake

" Culprit Fay," which he had composed in 1816, in proof of his assertion that the rivers of America were as well fitted for poetic treatment as the rivers of Scotland. In 1816 Irving had not yet published the first number of the " Sketch Book," which was to contain " Rip Van Winkle,"

## Abelard to Eloise

Weep on - weep on - we wail the dead -
  Now by those humid lids I swear,
For every tear of woe they shed
  My heart shall bleed a drop as dear.
Oh! tortures last convulsive sigh!
  Oh! all the pangs that wring the brow
When souls of guilt despairing die;
  Were heaven to what I suffer now.


Nay! look not thus - wert thou but blest,
  Erect & calm my soul could bear
To prison in this aching breast
  The writhings of its own despair -
The flame that sears my burning brain
  Should never force one stifled groan,
So I might take thy load of pain
  And bear its weary weight alone

88

the first attempt to give literary form to the legends of the Hudson; nor had Cooper then written the "Spy," the first American historical novel. Indeed, Cooper was one of those who then took part in the discussion, agreeing with Halleck that the streams of the New World lacked the romantic associations of the streams of the Old World. Drake stood up manfully for the poetic possibilities of America; and to support his challenge he composed in three days his exquisite poem.

Thus we see that the "Culprit Fay" was written as the "Pilot" was a few years later, not for its own sake only, but to be offered as evidence in behalf of an argument. Yet it does not by any labored structure reveal that its origin was deliberate and not spontaneous. No poem done of set purpose ever flowed more freely and more easily; and as we read its tuneful measures we never think of denying the right of the fairy folk to dwell on the beautiful banks of the Hudson. Nor did Drake in any way shirk the difficulties by trying to transplant to America all the traditional devices of European romance. He frankly introduced the insects of America, for example, and made them serve his picturesque purpose: —

> The winds are whist and the owl is still,
> The bat in the shelvy rock is hid,
> And naught is heard on the lonely hill
> But the cricket's chirp, and the answer shrill
> Of the gauze-winged katydid.

It was well for Drake that he did his work in youth, for when his life ended he was only twenty-five. Born in August, 1795, he died in September, 1820. He was, so Halleck declared, the handsomest man in New York. He was happily married. He had studied medicine and his practice as a physician was growing. He had high hopes for the future and thought but little of what he had already accomplished.    Halleck kept watch by the bedside of his dying friend ; and when Drake was dead, Halleck gave voice to his grief in the beautiful elegy, the opening lines of which are familiar to every lover of poetry : —

> Green be the turf above thee,
> Friend of my better days !
> None knew thee but to love thee,
> Nor named thee but to praise.

Halleck was five years older than Drake, whom he survived for nearly half a century.    Although he spent most of the years of his manhood in New York, Halleck was born in the village of Guilford, Connecticut, in 1790 ; and when he felt himself to be growing old he retired to his native place, and it was at Guilford that he died, in 1867.    His mother was descended from John Eliot, the apostle to the Indians. His father had been a Tory during the Revolution, and may even have served with the British troops.

Drake's Residence, Bowery, New York City

Perhaps it was from his father that Halleck derived his deference for British authority, and his liking for the

British system of society. Certainly he was not free from the taint of colonialism; he was wanting in the sturdy Americanism which was one of Drake's characteristics. Halleck looked across the ocean for light and leading; and the themes he treated were often European. It is significant that Drake's best known poem is that on the "American Flag," while the most popular poem of Halleck is "Marco Bozzaris."

Halleck's Residence, Guilford, Conn.

It was in 1826 that this resonant martial lyric was first published in the *New York Review*, then edited by Bryant. It has not a little of the swing and the fire and the power we find in the Grecian poems of Byron — and perhaps it owed something of its form and of its spirit to Byron's poetry. Halleck had also the knack of society verse; he could rime a gentle satire; he could make his stanzas brilliant and buoyant. The skill with which he handled meter has been highly praised by Bryant, who said that "in no poet could be found passages which flow with more sweet and liquid smoothness." He was witty rather than wise; he had abundant ease and a grace that seemed careless. He was apt in the adroit mingling of banter and sentiment, as in the lines on "Red Jacket," the Indian chief, and in the verses about "Wyoming." Sometimes the feeling expressed in his poems is sincere and strong, as in the lines on "Burns," although the expression itself is firmly kept from any suggestion of exuberance. Seldom were his stanzas as vigorous and direct as those on "Marco Bozzaris"; and rarely did he rise to the profound emotion of the poem he wrote after the death of Drake.

QUESTIONS. — What claims had New York in the first quarter of the nineteenth century to be considered the literary center of the United States ?

Tell how a discussion of that time led to the production of a celebrated poem.

Account for the oblivion into which the "Croaker" papers have now fallen.

What characteristics of Drake and Halleck are illustrated by the two most popular examples of their separate work ?

NOTE. — The poetical writings of Halleck, with extracts from those of Drake, have been edited by Gen. J. G. Wilson (D. Appleton & Co., $ 1.50).

Mr. Wilson is also the author of the "Life and Letters of Fitz-Greene Halleck" (D. Appleton & Co., $2.50), in which the brief career of Drake is also outlined.

## VIII  RALPH WALDO EMERSON

ALTHOUGH Franklin and Bryant were born in New England, they left it in early life — Franklin for Philadelphia, and Bryant for New York, where he found Irving and Cooper.  The earliest of the leaders of American literature to be born in New England, to live there, and to die there, was Ralph Waldo Emerson.

He is the foremost representative of the powerful influence which New England has exerted on American life and on American literature.  The fathers of Franklin and of Irving were newcomers ; the ancestors of Emerson had been settled in New England for five generations. They had been ministers of the gospel, one after another; and Emerson's grandfather belonged also to the church militant, urging on his parishioners to the fight at Concord Bridge in 1775, and dying in 1776 from a fever caught while on his way to join the troops at Ticonderoga.

Ralph Waldo Emerson was born May 25, 1803, in Boston, not far from the birthplace of Franklin. His father was a clergyman, who had recently founded what is now the library of the Boston Athenæum. Books, rather than the usual boyish sports, were the delight of the son. He rarely played, and never owned a sled. In the austere New England life of the time there was little leisure for mere amusement.

Emerson's father died before the boy was eight years old, and thereafter the child had to help his mother, who took boarders and tried hard to give her sons an education such as their father's. Emerson entered the Latin School in 1813, and one day the next year, when there was a rumor that the British were going to send a fleet to Boston Harbor, he went with the rest of the boys to help build earthworks on one of the islands. About this time, also, he began to rime, celebrating in juvenile verse the victories of the young American navy.

In August, 1817, Emerson entered Harvard College, obtaining the appointment of "President's Freshman," a student who received his lodgings free in return for carrying official messages. He served also as waiter at the college commons, and so saved three fourths the cost of his board. Later in his college course he acted as tutor to younger pupils. He seems to have impressed his instructors as a youth of remarkable ability; but he was not a diligent student.

In those days Harvard was not a university ; it was not even a college ; it was little more than a high school where boys recited their lessons. Emerson was only eighteen when he was graduated, feeling that the regular course of studies had done little for him, and having therefore strayed out of the beaten path to browse for himself among the books in the library. He was popular with the best of his classmates, and at graduation he was class poet.

Whatever may have been the value of a college educa- tion in those days, Emerson was the earliest of the little group of the founders of American literature to go through college. Franklin, having to work for his living from early boyhood, had no time ; Irving, after preparing for Colum- bia, threw his chance away ; Cooper was expelled from Yale ; and Bryant was so dissatisfied with Williams that he left it after a single year. But the authors who came after Emerson made sure of the best education that this country could afford them. Hawthorne and Longfellow were graduated from Bowdoin, while from Emerson's col- lege, Harvard, were to come Holmes and Lowell, Thoreau and Parkman.

When he graduated, Emerson's ambition was to be a professor of rhetoric ; but such a position was never offered to him. He taught school for a while in Boston, earning money to pay his debts and to help his mother. Then he entered the Divinity School at Harvard, and, in October, 1826, he was "approbated to preach," delivering his first sermon a few days later. For the sake of his health he spent that winter in Florida, at St. Augustine. On his return he lived chiefly in Cambridge, preaching here and there ; and in the spring of 1829 he became the minister of the old North Church in Boston. In September he married Miss Ellen Tucker, but he lost his wife soon after the marriage. Not long after, a change in his views as to religious rites and duties made him unwilling to remain in the ministry, and in 1832 he resigned his charge.

On Christmas day of that year he sailed for Europe in a small brig bound for Malta, whence he went over into Italy, and thence to France and Great Britain, and met the essayist Carlyle and the poets Wordsworth and Coleridge. With Carlyle Emerson formed a lasting friendship, which seems extraordinary, for few men were less akin in their manners or in their views of life. In low, clear tones the gentle American spoke to the soul of man, while the burly Scotch humorist was forever scolding and shrieking. Carlyle was proudly scornful and harshly indignant, while Emerson was kindly, tolerant, and forbearing; but different as were their attitudes, their aims were not so unlike, since Emerson loved good and Carlyle hated evil; and their friendship endured till death.

Toward the end of 1833 Emerson came back to America, pleased that in Europe he had met the men he most wished to see. A few months after his return he settled in Concord, to reside there for the rest of his life. In 1835 he married Miss Lidian Jackson, with whom he was to live happily for nearly half a century.

Emerson was now past thirty. He was not yet known as an author, and he did not look to authorship for his living; indeed, in the United States authorship could then give but a precarious livelihood. Besides, he preferred to teach by word of mouth. He still preached occasionally, and he lectured frequently. His earliest addresses seem to have been on scientific subjects, and he talked to his townsmen also about his travels in Europe, which was then distant at least a month's sail, and which few Americans could hope to visit. For many years he delivered in Boston, nearly every winter, long courses of lectures, not reported or printed, but containing much that the author repeated in the essays he was to publish afterward.

At last, in 1836, he put forth his first book, "Nature," and the next year he delivered an oration on "The Ameri-

Emerson's Residence, Concord, Mass.

can Scholar." Hitherto little had happened to him except the commonplaces of existence; thereafter, though his life remained tranquil, he was known to the world at large. He was greeted as are all who declare a new doctrine; welcomed by some, abused by many, misunderstood by most. Proclaiming the value of self-reliance, Emerson denounced man's slavery to his own worldly prosperity, and set forth at once the duty and the pleasure of the plain living which permits high thinking. "Why should you renounce your right to traverse the starlit deserts of truth," he asked, "for the premature comforts of an acre, house, and barn?"

He asserted the virtue of manual labor. Looking bravely toward the future, he bade his hearers break the bonds of the past. He told them to study themselves, since all the real good or evil that can befall must come from themselves. At the heart of Emerson's doctrine there was always a sturdy and wholesome Americanism.

He was never self-assertive. He never put himself forward ; and yet from that time on there was no denying his leadership of the intellectual advance of the United States. The most enlightened spirits of New England gathered about him ; and he found himself in the center of the vague movement known as "Transcendentalism." For all their hardness, the New Englanders are an imaginative race ; and Transcendentalism is but one of the waves of spiritual sentiment which have swept over them. Emerson himself had never a hint of eccentricity. His judgment was always sane and calm. He edited for a while the *Dial*, a magazine for which the Transcendentalists wrote, and which existed from 1840 to 1844. But he took no part in an experiment of communal life undertaken by a group of Transcendentalists at Brook Farm from 1841 to 1847. Among those who did join this community where all were to share in the labor of the field and of the • household were Nathaniel Hawthorne and George William Curtis.

In 1841 Emerson published the first volume of his "Essays"; and he sent forth a second series in 1844. In his hands the essay returns almost to the form of Montaigne and Bacon ; it is weighty and witty ; but it is not so light as it was with Addison and Steele, with Gold-smith and Irving. He indulged in fancies sometimes, and he strove to take his readers by surprise, to startle them, and so to arouse them to the true view of life. Nearly all his essays had been lectures, and every paragraph had been tested by its effect upon an audience. Thus the weak phrases were discarded one by one, until at last every sentence, polished by wear, rounded to a perfect sphere, went to the mark with unerring certainty.

To Emerson an essay was rather a collection of single sayings than a harmonious whole. He was keen-eyed and clear-sighted enough to understand his own shortcomings, and he once said that every sentence of his was an "infinitely repellent particle." His thoughts did not form a glittering chain; they were not even loosely linked together. They lay side by side like unset gems in a box. Emerson was rather a poet with moments of insight than a systematic philosopher. The lack of structure in his essays was, in a measure, due also to the way they were written.

It was Emerson's practice to set down in his journal his detached thoughts as soon as they had taken shape. Whenever he had a lecture to prepare, he selected from his journal those sentences which seemed to bear on the subject of his discourse, adding whatever other illustrations or anecdotes suggested themselves to him at the moment. "In writing my thoughts," he declared, "I seek no order, or harmony, or results. I am not careful to see how they comport with other thoughts and other words — I trust them for that — any more than how any one minute of the year is related to any other remote minute which yet I know is so related. The thoughts and the minutes obey their own magnetisms, and will certainly reveal themselves in time."

The ground-flames wash their ruby green,

The maple-tops their crimson tint,

On the poppy field each track is fair,

The fir's foot laves its mite print.

The pebble loosened from the path

Asks of the urchin to be tossed.

Thou flint ... able beats a heart,

The kind earth takes her children's hands

The Green lane is the schoolboy's friend,
Low leaves his quarrel apprehend;
The fresh ground loves his lithe obey,
The air rings forward to his call;
The brimming brook invites a leap,
He dives the hollow, climbs the steep,
The youth reads omens where he goes,
And speaks all languages the rose;

Emerson's first volume of "Poems" was published in 1846. Ten years before he had written the hymn sung at the completion of the monument commemorating Con- cord fight : —

> By the rude bridge that arched the flood,
> Their flag to April's breeze unfurled,
> Here once the embattled farmers stood,
> And fired the shot heard round the world.

This is one of the best, and one of the best known, of the poems of American patriotism. But Emerson cared too little for form often to write so perfect a poem. The bonds of rime and meter irked him and he broke them willfully. Now and again he happened on a quatrain than which nothing can be more beautiful : —

> Thou canst not wave thy staff in air,
> Or dip thy paddle in the lake,
> But it carves the bow of beauty there,
> And the ripples in rimes the oar forsake.

Following Bryant and Drake, Emerson put into his verse nature as he saw it about him — the life of American woods and fields. No second-hand nightingale sang in his verses ; he took pleasure in riming the "Humble-bee" and the "Titmouse," and in singing the streams and the hills of New England. Herein there was no lack of elevation. The spirit of the true poet Emerson had abundantly ; indeed, there are those now who call him a poet rather than a philosopher. However careless his verse making —and it was sometimes very slovenly — the best of his stanzas are strong and bracing ; they lift up the heart of man.

One of Emerson's poems most richly laden with emotion and experience is the "Threnody," which he wrote after the death of his first-born. He was a fond father; and his home life was beautiful, like that of nearly all the foremost American authors. He liked children, and they liked him. He understood them, entering into their feelings as easily as he entered into their sports. In his own family, discipline — never neglected — was enforced by the gentlest methods; and he had unbounded interest in the details of the school life of his own children, getting them to talk to him as freely as they did to their comrades. This was but an example of his willingness always to put himself in the place of others and to try to see things from their point of view. An instance of this sympathetic faculty, and of his abiding simplicity, was his comment on the minister who went up to the pulpit after Emerson had lectured, and who prayed that they might be delivered from ever again hearing such "transcendental nonsense." Emerson listened to this, and remarked quietly, " He seems a very conscientious, plain-spoken man."

In 1847 Emerson made a second voyage to Europe, sailing in October and coming home in July of the following year. The most of the time he spent in England, lecturing often, meeting the most distinguished men and women of Great Britain, studying matters and men in the little island. In the summer he crossed the Channel to France, and saw Paris in the heat of the revolution of 1848. After his return to America he resumed his lecturing, pushing as far west as the Mississippi.

Certain of the lectures prepared for delivery in England supplied the material for his next book — "Representative Men " — published in 1850. Only two of Emerson's books have any singleness of scheme, and this is one of them. He discusses first the uses of great men, and then he considers in turn Plato, Swedenborg, Montaigne, Shakspere, Napoleon, and Goethe — great men, all of them, interesting in themselves and doubly interesting as Emerson reflects their images in his clear mirror. It is instructive to contrast Emerson's hopeful and helpful treatment of these "Representative Men" with Carlyle's doleful and robustious writing upon the kindred topic of "Heroes and Hero Worship."

The observations Emerson had made of English life during his two visits had been used in various lectures, and from these he made a book, published in 1856, under the title of "English Traits." For close argument he had no fitness and no liking, but this volume has more logical sequence than any other of his. It may be said almost to have a plan. It opens with a narrative of his first voyage to England, and it contains a study of the character of the British. It is perhaps the best book ever written about a great people by a foreigner.

Emerson had a singularly keen sense of the ridiculous, he had an uncommon share of common sense, and he had a marvelous insight into humanity; and it is therefore the highest possible testimony to the substantial merits of the British that they stood so well the ordeal of his examination. He was too sturdy an American to be taken in by the glamour of the aristocratic arrangement of their society; he saw clearly the weakness of the British system, but he is never hostile, and never patronizing; he is always ready to praise boldly.

The spirit of the book can be shown by the extract from a letter he wrote to a friend in America just before his return : "I leave England with increased respect for the Englishman, . . . the more generous that I have no sympathy for him." Emerson expressed his admiration heartily, but he rejoiced always that he lived in a society free from the traditions of feudalism.

In his own country he was a good citizen, taking part
in town meeting, and doing his share of town work — even
accepting his election as a hogreeve of Concord.   Declaring always the duty and the dignity of labor, he detested
the system of slavery under which white men were sup-
ported by the toil of black men.   He did not join the
abolitionists, but his voice was strong on the side of freedom.   He spoke out plainly during the strife in Kansas,
and again after the hanging of John Brown.   Yet he was
like Goethe in finding patriotism too narrow for him : he
looked forward and he foresaw the Brotherhood of Man.
But no intensely national poet, no Hugo, no Tennyson,
was more stimulating to his country.   He it was who had
edged the resolve of the American people when the hour
came for stern battle.   Lowell said that to Emerson more
than to all other causes "the young martyrs of our Civil
War owe the sustaining strength of thoughtful heroism
that is so touching in every record of their lives."

When the war came at last, Emerson was unfailingly
hopeful.   He delivered an address on the Emancipation
Proclamation, declaring the young happy in that they then
found the pestilence of slavery cleansed out of the earth.
On New Year's Day, 1863, he read his noble "Boston
Hymn," with its rough and resonant verses ; and in the
same year he wrote the "Voluntaries," wherein we find
this lofty and inspiring quatrain : —

> So nigh is grandeur to our dust,
> So near is God to man,
> When Duty whispers low, *Thou must,*
> The youth replies, *I can.*

And at the meeting held at Concord in memory of
Abraham Lincoln, he made a short address in which he

set forth the character of the fallen leader with the utmost sympathy and the clearest insight.

A collection of Emerson's later essays had been published in 1860 under the title of the first of them, the "Conduct of Life"; and in 1870 another collection followed, also named after the opening paper, "Society and Solitude." There can be found in these volumes the same wit and paradox, the same felicity of phrase, the same beauty of thought, the same elevation of spirit, that we find in his earlier volumes.

Emerson grew but little as he became older; he was at the end very much what he was at the beginning. He admitted his own "incapacity for methodical writing." However inspiring, every sentence stands by itself; the paragraphs might be rearranged almost at random without loss to the essential value of the essays. Emerson made no effort to formulate his doctrine; he had no compact system of philosophy. Perhaps he was not a philosopher in the strict sense of the word; but rather a maker of golden sayings, full of vital suggestion, to help men to be themselves and to make the utmost of themselves.

For years Emerson had extended his winter lecturing tours as far west as the Mississippi; and in 1871 he accepted the invitation of a friend to visit California, bearing the fatigue of the long journey with unwearied cheerfulness. Toward the end of 1872 he sailed for Europe, on a third visit to the Old World. In England and France and Italy he met again his friends of former years, and he wandered on as far as Egypt, where he had never been before. He was back again in Concord the next spring, and his return home was marked by an outpouring of all his townsmen to welcome him among them once more.

For several years Emerson had written but little, although he continued now and then to draw out new essays and make addresses from the store of lectures he had by him. Thus in 1870 he had given a course of university lectures at Harvard on the "Natural History of the Intellect," and in 1878 he read a lecture on the "Fortune of the Republic," written and already delivered in war time fifteen years before. And in 1875 yet another collection of his essays was published under the title of the first paper, "Letters and Social Aims." This volume had been prepared for the press by an old friend, for Emerson's powers were beginning to fail. He retained possession of his faculties to the last; but though his mind was clear, he had increasing difficulty in recalling the words to express his ideas. He forgot not only proper names, but even the names of common things, while keeping the power of describing them in the words he had left. So, when he wanted to say "umbrella" once, and was unable to recall the name, he said, "I can't tell its name, but I can tell its history. Strangers take it away." Emerson looked calmly forward to death, and it came when he was nearly seventy-nine years of age, on April 27, 1882.

Benjamin Franklin, born in Boston almost a century before Ralph Waldo Emerson was born there, lived long enough to see the straggling colonies with their scant four hundred thousand settlers grow into a vigorous young nation of four million inhabitants. Emerson, born only thirteen years after Franklin's death, lived long enough to see the United States increase to thirty-eight, and a population of five and a half millions expand to a population of fifty millions. He survived to behold a little nation grow to be a mighty people, able to fight a righteous war without flinching.

Different as they are, Franklin and Emerson are both typical Americans — taken together they give us the two sides of the American character. Franklin stands for the real, and Emerson for the ideal. Franklin represents the prose of American life, and Emerson the poetry. Franklin's power is limited by the bounds of common sense, while Emerson's appeal is to the wider imagination. Where Emerson advises you to "hitch your wagon to a star," Franklin is ready with an improved axle-grease for the wheels. Franklin declares that honesty is the best policy; and Emerson insists on honesty as the only means whereby a man may be free to undertake higher things. Self-reliance was at the core of the doctrine of each of them, but one urged self-help in the material world and the other in the spiritual. Hopeful they were, both of them, and kindly, and shrewd; and in the making of the American people, in the training and in the guiding of this immense population, no two men have done more than these two sons of New England.

QUESTIONS. — Compare the antecedents of Emerson with those of several earlier American authors.

Speak of Emerson's boyhood and student days, and of his choice of a profession.

How did the year 1833 influence Emerson's later life?

How did Emerson become the leader of advanced thought in America?

What may be said of Emerson as an essayist? And as a poet?

Show how Emerson, in two books that grew out of his second visit to Europe, displayed the breadth of his sympathies.

Discuss the quality of Emerson's patriotism.

What evidence do you find in Emerson's later books to show the early maturing of his mind?

Describe the last years of Emerson's life.

Compare Emerson and Franklin as typical Americans.

NOTE. — The only complete edition of Emerson's works is that published by Houghton, Mifflin & Co. (12 vols., $1.25 or $1.75 each). The poems are contained in one volume of the Household Edition ($1.50). It is best to beware of unauthorized editions of the poems, none of which are complete. There are now cheap editions of certain of the earlier volumes of essays. The "American Scholar," "Self-Reliance," and "Compensation" are included in a single volume (American Book. Company, 20 cents). The "American Scholar and other American Addresses" forms one number of the Riverside Literature series (Houghton, Mifflin & Co., 15 cents).

There are biographies by J. Elliot Cabot, Dr. Richard Garnett, Alexander Ireland, E. W. Emerson, and in American Men of Letters series by Dr. Holmes (Houghton, Mifflin & Co., $1.25).

For criticism, see Lowell's "Fable for Critics" and "Emerson the Lecturer" (in "My Study Windows") ; Mr. E. C. Stedman (in "American Poets") ; and G. W. Curtis (in "Literary and Social Essays") ; Mr. John Burroughs (in "Indoor Studies") ; and Prof. Richardson (in his history of "American Literature"). For an account of the Transcendental movement and of the Brook Farm experiment, see Frothingham's "Life of George Ripley" in American Men of Letters series, and his history of "Transcendentalism in New England."

## IX  NATHANIEL HAWTHORNE

THE little town of Salem in Massachusetts is memorable chiefly because of the pitiful witchcraft trials held there two hundred years ago.   One of the judges most active in the task of convicting the poor creatures then accused of evil practices was John Hathorne.   In Salem there lived, first and last, six generations of this family (spelling its name sometimes Hathorne and sometimes Hawthorne); and in Salem Judge Hathorne's grandson's grandson was born in 1804 on the Fourth of July — a fitting birthday for an author so intensely American as Nathaniel Hawthorne.

Four years after the boy's birth, his father, a sea captain, died at Surinam; and his mother never recovered from the blow of her husband's death, withdrawing herself wholly from society, and living for forty years the life of a recluse, even to the extent of taking her meals apart from her children.

When Nathaniel Hawthorne was eight or nine years old his mother took up her residence on the banks of Sebago Lake in Maine, where the family owned a large tract of land. Here the boy ran wild, fishing and swimming, shooting and skating — and, on the rainy days, reading. This life in the woods increased the liking for solitude which he inherited from his mother, and which in after years he was never able wholly to overcome. In time he went back to Salem to prepare for college. In 1821, being then seventeen, he entered Bowdoin, having Long-

Hawthorne's Birthplace, Salem, Mass.

fellow for a classmate, and making a close friend of Franklin Pierce, who was in the class before him and who was afterward President of the United States.

He was graduated in 1825, and he then went back to Salem. The family was fairly well-to-do, and it was not needful for Nathaniel to hurry in choosing a profession. He had already decided that he wished to be an author, but authorship offered little chance of a livelihood. There was not then a single prosperous magazine in the United States. Yet the "Sketch Book" and the "Spy," the pioneers of American literature, had been published not five years before; and the success of Irving and of Cooper, and the prompt appreciation with which their early writings were received both in America and in England, was encouraging to other native authors. So the year after he left college Hawthorne wrote a tale and published it at his own expense; but it made no impression on the public, and very few copies were sold.

The tale appeared without the author's name, and its failure seems to have increased Hawthorne's love of solitude. For ten years and more he lived in his mother's house almost as alone as if he were a hermit in a cave. For months together he scarcely met any one outside of his own family, seldom going out save at twilight or to take the nearest way to the desolate seashore. Once a year, or thereabouts (so he told a friend a long while after), he used to make an excursion of a few weeks, "in which I enjoyed as much of life as other people do in the whole year's round." Unnatural as this existence was, Hawthorne kept his health and seldom lost his cheerfulness. He read endlessly and he wrote unceasingly. These were his 'prentice years of authorship; and in them he became a master of the craft of writing.

Most of his early attempts at fiction he burned; but in time his hand became surer, and he found that he had learned at last the difficult art of story telling. His little tales began to be published here and there in monthlies and in annuals. Being anonymous, or under differing signatures, they did not attract attention to the author; but in the newspaper notices of the periodicals in which they appeared, they were often picked out for praise.

This finally encouraged Hawthorne to gather a score of them into a single volume published in 1837 under the

apt title of "Twice-Told Tales." Although the little book
had no remarkable sale, it won its way steadily; and the
readers who had enjoyed Irving's pleasant sketches of
New York character in "Rip Van Winkle" and the
"Legend of Sleepy Hollow" could not but remark that
Hawthorne's pictures of New England character revealed
a stronger imagination and a deeper insight into human
nature. Delightful as was Irving's writing, Hawthorne
had a richer style and a firmer grasp of the art of fiction.
After the publication of this collection of short stories,
Hawthorne ceased to be what he once called himself —
"the obscurest man of letters in America." His classmate Longfellow, with whom he had not been intimate
in college, reviewed the book with hearty commendation.
Hawthorne wrote him that hitherto there had "been no
warmth of approbation, so that I have always written with
benumbed fingers." Now at last he basked in the sunshine
of public approval, and he was encouraged to go on with his
writing. Yet it was five years before his next book was
issued, and even then the new volume was only a second
series of "Twice-Told Tales," collected from the periodicals.
But meanwhile he had come out into the world again,
and mixed once more with his fellow-men. He had edited
a magazine for a few months; he had held a place for two
years in the Boston customhouse; he had been one of
those who formed a settlement at Brook Farm; and he
had married Miss Sophia Peabody. The marriage took
place in 1842, and the young couple moved to Concord.
They went to live in the house which had been built for
Emerson's grandfather, and in which Emerson himself
had dwelt ten years before. Hawthorne took for his study
the room in this old manse in which Emerson had written
"Nature"; and in that room, during the next few years,

he wrote stories and sketches which were collected into the two volumes published in 1846 as "Mosses from an Old Manse."

These tales are like those in Hawthorne's earlier collections, but they are unlike any stories ever written anywhere else by anybody else. They are strangely interesting, all of them; they are novel, varied, and ingenious; they are full of fancy; and they have often an allegory hidden within, and a profound moral also, never obtruded,

The Old Manse

but to be found easily by all who take the trouble to seek it. Here may be the best place to note that these same qualities, ripened, perhaps, and enriched by experience, are to be found again in Hawthorne's final collection of tales made six years later, and called, after the first of them, the "Snow Image."

Hawthorne was happier in these years of manhood than he had been in his youth. It might almost be said that his marriage was the making of him; for that had brought him back into the world before it was too late — before the doors of solitude were closed upon him forever. Yet these early years of wedded life were a time of struggle; for he had lost money, and had little to live on.

Knowing his need of an assured income to bring up his young family, some of his friends in 1846 secured his appointment as surveyor of the port of Salem, the town where he had been born about forty years before. He remained in the customhouse for three years, with increasing dislike for the work; and then he was suddenly removed to make a place for a politician.

When he went home one day, earlier than usual, and told his wife that he had lost his place, she exclaimed: "Oh, then you can write your book!" And when he asked what they were to live on while he was writing this book, she showed him the money she had been saving up, week by week, out of their household expenses.

That very afternoon he sat down and began to write the more serious work of fiction he had longed for leisure to attempt. It was really the first book he had written since the forgotten and unknown romance. The other volumes he had published were but collections of tales, while this was to be a story long enough to stand by itself. A broader experience is needed to compose a full-grown novel than to sketch a short story, and the great novelists have often essayed their first elaborate fictions when no longer young. Scott was more than forty when he published the first of the Waverley novels; Thackeray was not far from forty when "Vanity Fair" was finished; George Eliot was almost forty when "Adam Bede" appeared; and Hawthorne was forty-six when he sent forth the "Scarlet Letter" in 1850.

With the striking exception of "Uncle Tom's Cabin," no American work of fiction has had the quick and lasting popularity of the "Scarlet Letter"; and while Mrs. Stowe's story owed much of its success to the public interest in the slavery question, Hawthorne's romance had no such outside aid. Hawthorne's study of the Puritan life in New England is superior to Mrs. Stowe's novel. It is a masterpiece of narrative, every incident being so aptly chosen, so skillfully prepared, so well placed, that it seems a necessary result of the situation. Since the "Scarlet Letter" was written half a century has passed, and many books highly praised when it was first published are now left unread; but Hawthorne's great story stands to-day higher than ever before in the esteem of those best fitted to judge.

The author thought that the romance was too somber, and he relieved it with a humorous sketch of his life in the Salem customhouse. The reading public gave the book so hearty a welcome that Hawthorne was warmed out of his chilly solitude. For the first time he tasted popularity, and it did him good. He moved to Lenox, and there he wrote a second long story, less solemn than the first, brisker and brighter, and yet not without the same solid and serious merits. The "House of the Seven Gables" was published in 1851. It is rather a romance than a novel; and in it the author allowed his humor more play than had been becoming in the "Scarlet Letter." Like that, the new story was a study of the life the author best knew. How well he knew it may be judged from Lowell's declaration that the "House of the Seven Gables" is "the most valuable contribution to New England history that has yet been made."

A true historian Hawthorne might be in his understanding of the conditions of life in the old colony days, and of the feelings of the men and women who then walked the streets of Salem ; but a story teller he was above all else — a teller of tales to whom every lover of literature could not but listen eagerly. And in the next volume he made ready for the press he presented himself simply as a teller of tales. The "Wonder Book for Girls and Boys," written in the same year as the "House of the Seven Gables," is the book which has most endeared Hawthorne to American children, who have been charmed with the ease and the grace with which he set forth anew the marvelous myths of antiquity.

In the "Wonder Book" he retold the legends of the "Gorgon's Head" and the "Three Golden Apples" and the "Chimæra," and in "Tanglewood Tales" (which was published two or three years later, but which may be considered as a second volume of the "Wonder Book") he described the adventures of those who went forth to seek the "Golden Fleece," to explore the labyrinth of the "Minotaur," and to sow the "Dragon's Teeth."

His next story for grown-up people was called the "Blithedale Romance," and it was published in 1852. It was derived more or less closely from the memory of his own experiences a few years before at Brook Farm, where a little group of reformers and men of letters, led astray for a moment by some of the notions of the time, sought to simplify their lives by doing themselves the rough work of a New England farm. The most valuable result of this experiment is perhaps Hawthorne's story ; and that story is generally held to be the least interesting and the least satisfactory of all that Hawthorne wrote.  Here, indeed, was the instance where he was not fortunate in his choice of a subject.

In the year the "Blithedale Romance" was published Hawthorne went back once more to Concord; and there he bought the house of Mr. Alcott, the father of the author of "Little Women."  This house he called "The Wayside," and it was the home of the family until Hawthorne's death.  But they did not live in it long at first. One of the candidates for the presidency of the United States was Hawthorne's college friend, Franklin Pierce, for whom he prepared a campaign biography — just as Mr. Howells in 1876 wrote the life of Hayes when he was a candidate for the presidency.  When Pierce became President he appointed Nathaniel Hawthorne consul to Liverpool, England, one of the best-paid offices under the government.  Hawthorne lived in England for four years; and then he made a journey to France, Switzerland, and Italy, lingering in Rome long enough to gather materials for a new story, and returning in 1859 to England to write it.

This new story, published early in 1860, was the "Marble Faun, a Romance of Monte Beni" (known in England as "Transformation," because the British publisher chose to change the title).  It was a tale of life in Italy. The beauty of the story is felt by all its readers, and its power cannot be denied.  But the book abounds in shadowy suggestions; and some of its outlines are so misty that we are still a little in doubt as to what did happen to all of the characters.  Never before had Hawthorne been more skillfully mysterious; and never before had the magic of his manner been more charming to his readers.

I went ... deliberately dressed, and ... well, ... on horseback, travelling on his own hook, calling for oats and ... "Shop of ... by and walk- ... at the bar — like any other Christian. Of ... men from Christian ... stated. "I wished I had a thousand ... the clause ... Alabama." "I made a speedy retreat from ... — the ... very ... to Heaven — and to talk of ... & ... like him.

Left North Adams, Sept 11th. } 1838.
Reached Home. Sept 24th.

Nath. Hawthorne.

119

Perhaps the vagueness of this story was the result of its scene being laid upon a foreign soil, whereon Hawthorne did not feel himself absolutely at home. At the very time he was planning the "Marble Faun" he recorded in his notebook that "it needs the native air to give life a reality." Despite its hazily hinted plot, the "Marble Faun" is cherished by Hawthorne's admirers as second only to the "Scarlet Letter." And, as it happened, it was the last of his romances he was to live long enough to complete.

The Wayside

In 1860 Hawthorne returned to his native air, settling down in "The Wayside" at Concord. He planted trees, laid out walks, enlarged the house, and made himself at home. He had a theme for a new romance; and this he sketched out two or three times, and differently every time, but never to his own satisfaction.

Failing to get the strange subject of this proposed tale into the perfect form he sought, Hawthorne turned from it for a while. He had always kept a journal, writing in it freely when the mood was on him, setting down suggestions for stories, recording visits and conversations, and describing people and places. From this storehouse he now selected passages concerning England and the English, and these he wove into a series of delightful chapters, published in 1863. The title which Hawthorne gave to these collected papers was "Our Old Home"—and the title itself was an evidence of the kindly and fraternal feeling of Americans toward the elder branch of the race. This same gentle liking inspired the English pages of Irving's "Sketch Book"; and it also controlled the criticism in Emerson's acute "English Traits."

After the publication of this volume of descriptive papers, Hawthorne returned to his story, and finally managed to write the earlier chapters. But his health was failing fast, and he was not able to finish what he had begun. He made several little journeys in search of relief; and it was on one of these, a trip to the White Mountains with Franklin Pierce, that he died. His death took place at Plymouth, New Hampshire, a little before midnight on May 18, 1864; and on the twenty-third he was buried at Concord in the cemetery called "Sleepy Hollow."

Emerson and Longfellow, Lowell and Whittier, were at the funeral. Longfellow wrote in his diary: "It was a lovely day; the village all sunshine and blossoms and the song of birds. You cannot imagine anything at once more sad and beautiful. He is buried on a hilltop under the pines."

And this funeral of his classmate suggested to Longfellow one of his most tender poems:—

Now I look back, and meadow, manse, and stream
  Dimly my thought defines ;
I only see — a dream within a dream —
  The hilltop hearsed with pines.

          *    *    *    *    *    *

There in seclusion and remote from men
  The wizard hand lies cold,
Which at its topmost speed let fall the pen,
  And left the tale half told.

At intervals since Hawthorne's death all the writings he left behind him have been published, one after another — his private letters, the notebooks he kept irregularly in America and in Europe, and the several efforts he made to shape the story he finally left unfinished when he died. But the publication of these things never intended for the public has not interfered with his fame. Though they did not add to it, they did not detract from it. They took us in some measure into his workshop, but they could not reveal the secret of his art : that died with him. They showed that his English was always pure and clear, and that his style was always simple and noble. They revealed little or nothing of real value for an estimate of the author, though they served to confirm the belief that he brooded long over his tales and his romances, shaping each to the inward moral it was to declare, and perfecting each slowly until it had attained in every detail the symmetry which should satisfy his own most exacting taste.

Many have marveled that Hawthorne should have been able to write romances here in this new country of ours, which seems to lack all that others have considered needful for romance ; but to a seer of his insight this was no difficult matter. Hawthorne was able to find romance not in external trappings and picturesque fancy costumes, but deep down in the soul of man himself.

Beside this power of entering into the recesses of the human heart, he had not only a vigorous imagination, not only great ingenuity in inventing incident, not only the gift of the story-telling faculty in a high degree, but also a profound respect for the art of narrative ; and these qualities all combined to make him the most accomplished artist in fiction that America has yet produced.

QUESTIONS. — What can you say of the Hawthorne family; of Nathaniel Hawthorne's early life and of his education?

Describe Hawthorne's life during his early years of authorship.

What characteristics of Hawthorne's writings enabled him to find a growing audience among the admirers of Irving and Cooper?

How was Hawthorne brought back into the world before the doors of solitude were closed upon him forever?

How did he find the opportunity to begin the work of his life?

Compare the "Scarlet Letter" with the only American work of fiction which has had as quick and lasting a popularity as it has enjoyed.

Tell how he succeeded in interesting children in one of his works.

How did Hawthorne suddenly find his course of life turned in a new direction ?

How may Hawthorne's life for the next few years account for the shadowy character of the most skillfully mysterious of his stories?

What evidence may the reader of Hawthorne find in his works that he shared the sentiments of at least two other famous American writers toward the elder branch of the English-speaking race?

What qualities combined to make Hawthorne the greatest American writer of fiction that has yet appeared?

NOTE. — The only complete editions of Hawthorne's works are those issued by Houghton, Mifflin & Co. (Popular edition, 8 vols., $12. Riverside edition, with notes by Mr. G. P. Lathrop, 13 vols., $26). Certain of the earlier books can now be had in cheap editions.

There are biographies by Mr. .G. P. Lathrop, Mr. Henry James, Mr. Julian Hawthorne, and Mr. M. D. Conway.

For criticism, see G. W. Curtis (in " Literary and Social Studies ") ; Mr. T. W. Higginson (in " Short Studies of American Authors ") ; Mr. Leslie Stephen (in " Hours in a Library ") ; Prof. C. F. Richardson (in his history of " American Literature ") ; and Mr. W. D. Howells (in " My Literary Passions ").

## X   HENRY WADSWORTH LONGFELLOW

In the first ten years of the nineteenth century, there were born in New England five of the foremost authors of America.   Emerson and Hawthorne were respectively four and three years older than Longfellow.   Whittier and Holmes were respectively ten months and two years younger.   As they grew up and began to write, and got to know one another, these authors became friends; and their friendship lasted with their lives.   One after another they all gained fame; and although not the greatest of the five, perhaps, Longfellow was always the most popular.   Not merely in the United States and Great Britain, but in Canada and Australia and India, and wherever the English language is spoken, there were readers in plenty for the gentle, the manly, the beautiful verses of Longfellow.

His mother's father had been a general in the Revolutionary army. His mother's brother (after whom he was named) had been an officer in the American navy, losing his life in Preble's attack on Tripoli. His father, once a member of Congress, was one of the leading lawyers of Portland. And it was in that pleasant Maine city that Henry Wadsworth Longfellow was born, on February 27, 1807. There he passed his childhood. There he got that liking for the sea and for ships and for sailors which was to give a salt-water savor to so many of his ballads. There, as he grew to boyhood, he

Longfellow's Birthplace

browsed amid the books of his father's ample library, feeling his love for literature steadily growing.

He was a schoolboy of twelve when the first numbers of Irving's "Sketch Book" appeared, and he read it "with ever-increasing wonder and delight, spellbound by its pleasant humor, its melancholy tenderness, its atmosphere of reverie." A few months before the "Sketch Book" began, Bryant had published his "Thanatopsis," and others of his earlier poems followed soon ; so the schoolboy in Portland came under the influence of Bryant's poetry almost at the same time that he felt the charm of Irving's prose.    When he was only thirteen the young Longfellow began to write verses of his own, some of which were printed in the newspapers.   He was only fourteen when he passed the entrance examinations of Bowdoin College, where he was to have Hawthorne as a classmate.

Long before his college course was over he had made up his mind to become a man of letters.   In his last year at Bowdoin, being then eighteen, he wrote to his father : " I most eagerly aspire after future eminence in literature ; my whole soul burns ardently for it, and every earthly thought centers in it."   But here in America, in 1825, no man could hope to support himself by prose and verse.

Fortunately just then a professorship of modern languages was founded in Bowdoin, and the position was offered to Longfellow, with permission to spend several years in Europe fitting himself for his duties.   He accepted eagerly ; and his sojourn in France and Spain, in Italy and Germany, made him master of the four great European languages with their marvelous literatures.   He studied hard and wrote little while he was away.   At last, in 1829, being then twenty-two, he returned to his native land and settled down to teach his fellow-countrymen what he had learned abroad.

In 1831 he married Miss Mary Potter.   In addition to his work in the college, he found time to write critical articles on foreign literature.   He seems to have had but few poetic impulses at this period ; and his thoughts expressed themselves more naturally in prose.   The influence of Irving is visible in a series of rambling travel sketches, finally revised for publication as a book in 1833, under the title " Outre-Mer : a Pilgrimage beyond the Sea."   It has not a little of the charm of the " Sketch Book," with a

deeper poetic grace of its own and a more romantic touch.
The year after this first venture into literature, Longfellow was called to the professorship of modern languages at Harvard College.   Again he went to Europe
for further study, being absent for a year and a half;
but his journey was saddened by the death of his wife.
Toward the end of 1836 he took up his abode in Cambridge, where he was to reside for the rest of his life — for

Longfellow's Residence. Cambridge, Mass.

forty-five years.   He was made to feel at home in the
society of the scholars who clustered about Harvard, then
almost the sole center of culture in the country.
   His work for the college was not so exacting that he
had not time for literature.   The impulse to write poetry
returned; yet the next book he published was the prose
"Hyperion," which appeared in 1839, and which, though
it has little plot or action, may be called a romance.   The

youthful and poetic hero, a passionate pilgrim in Europe, was, more or less, a reflection of Longfellow himself.

A few months later, in the same year, he published his first volume of poetry — "Voices of the Night," in which he reprinted certain of his earlier verses, most of them written while he was at Bowdoin. Some of these boyish verses show the influence of Bryant, and others reveal to us that the young poet had not yet looked at life for himself, but still saw it through the stained-glass windows of European tradition. The same volume contained also some more recent poems: the "Beleaguered City," and the "Reaper and the Flowers," and the "Psalm of Life" — perhaps the first of his poems to win a swift and abiding popularity. These lyrics testified that Longfellow was beginning to have a style of his own. As Hawthorne wrote to him, "Nothing equal to them was ever written in this world — this western world, I mean."

Certainly no American author had yet written any poem of the kind so good as the best of those in Longfellow's volume of "Ballads" printed two years later. Better than any other American poet Longfellow had mastered the difficulties of the story in song; and he knew how to combine the swiftness and the picturesqueness the ballad requires. His ballads have more of the old-time magic, more of the early simplicity, than those of any other modern English author. Of its kind, there is nothing better in the language than the "Skeleton in Armor," with its splendid lyric swing; and the "Village Blacksmith" and the "Wreck of the 'Hesperus'" are almost as good in their humble sphere. "Excelsior," in the same volume, voices the noble aspirations of youth, and has been taken to heart by thousands of boys and girls.

He went to Europe again in 1842 for his health ; and on the voyage home he wrote eight " Poems on Slavery," which he published soon after he landed. The next year he married Miss Frances Appleton. About the same time he published the "Spanish Student," a play not intended for the theater, and lacking the dramatic action the stage demands. Neither the " Poems on Slavery " nor the "Spanish Student" showed him at his best ; but three years after the latter he published the "Belfry of Bruges," in which were to be found more than one of his finest poems, among them the "Old Clock on the Stairs " and the " Arsenal at Springfield."

Longfellow wrote a cordial review of Hawthorne's "Twice-Told Tales," and it was from Hawthorne that he heard the pathetic legend of the two Acadian lovers parted on their marriage morn, when the people of the French province were shipped away by the British authorities. " If you do not want this incident for a tale, let me have it for a poem," he said ; and Hawthorne willingly gave it up.

This was the germ of " Evangeline," which Longfellow published in 1847, and which was accepted at once as his masterpiece. It was the most beautiful and the most touching tale in verse yet told by any American poet ; and its charm was increased greatly by the skill with which the natural scenery of America, and our varying seasons, were used to furnish a background before which the simple figures of the story moved with fidelity to life. Even the strange proper names were invested with magic.

In 1849 Longfellow published his last prose book, " Kavanagh," a dreamy tale which Hawthorne hailed as a true picture of life — "as true as those reflections of the trees and banks that I used to see in Concord ; but refined to a higher degree than they, as if the reflection were itself reflected." The next year he gathered into a volume called the "Seaside and the Fireside" a score of short poems, including the "Fire of Driftwood" and the "Building of the Ship." With the sea as a subject, Longfellow had always a double share of inspiration, for he had retained in manhood his boyish love for the deep, and his sympathetic understanding of its mysteries.

As his poetic powers ripened and won prompt recognition, the daily labor of the classroom became more irksome to him, and at last, in 1854, he resigned his professorship. But he continued to reside in Cambridge, dwelling in the Craigie House, which had been Washington's headquarters. Longfellow's father-in-law had bought the house for him, and it is now known as the Longfellow House. The cultivated society of the little town was very congenial, and he had many friends in Boston and in Concord.

Like all true artists, he was greatly interested in his craft, and was fond of verse-making experiments. He had a delicate ear, and he felt the fitness of certain measures for certain themes. For "Evangeline" he chose a form of verse suggested by the verse of the "Iliad" and the "Æneid"; and how well this suited his subject can be seen by reading this description of the song of the mocking-bird : —

Then from a neighboring thicket the mocking-bird, wildest of singers,
Swinging aloft on a willow spray that hung o'er the water,
Shook from his little throat such floods of delirious music,
That the whole air and the woods and the waves seemed silent to
    listen.
Plaintive at first were the tones and sad ; then soaring to madness
Seemed they to follow or guide the revel of frenzied Bacchantes.
Single notes were then heard, in sorrowful low lamentation ;
Till, having gathered them all, he flung them abroad in derision,

As when, after a storm, a gust of wind through the tree-tops
Shakes down the rattling rain in a crystal shower on the branches.

Now compare the same description as Longfellow himself
rewrote it in the customary rimed couplets : —

> Upon a spray that overhung the stream,
> The mocking-bird, awaking from his dream,
> Poured such delirious music from his throat
> That all the air seemed listening to his note.
> Plaintive at first the song began, and slow ;
> It breathed of sadness, and of pain and woe ;
> Then, gathering all his notes, abroad he flung
> The multitudinous music from his tongue, —
> As, after showers, a sudden gust again
> Upon the leaves shakes down the rattling rain.

In his next long poem Longfellow attempted another
new meter, borrowed from the old Finnish poets. He was
always interested in the American Indian, and one of his
earliest poems was the "Burial of the Minnisink," as one
of his latest was the "Revenge of Rain-in-the-face." He
now decided that the mythical legends of the red men could
be woven into a poem of which an Indian should be the
central figure. The simple rhythm was exactly suited to
the simple story. "Hiawatha" was published in 1855, and
its instant success surpassed that of "Evangeline," which
was its only rival among the longer poems of American
authors upon a peculiarly American subject. The easy
verses sang themselves into the memory of all who read
the poem ; and the descriptions of nature delighted all
who had kept their eyes open as they walked through our
American woods and fields.

Encouraged by the hearty welcome given to these two
American poems, Longfellow, in 1858, published a third,
the "Courtship of Miles Standish." In this he told no

pathetic tale of parted lovers, nor did he draw on the quaint lore of the red men; he took his story from the annals of his own ancestors, the sturdy founders of New England. As it happened, he himself (like his fellow-poet, Bryant) was a direct descendant of John Alden and Priscilla, the Puritan maiden whose wooing he narrated. The "Courtship of Miles Standish" is only less popular than its predecessors, "Evangeline" and "Hiawatha"; all three have been taken to heart by the American people; all were composed during the brightest years of the poet's life, when his family were growing up about him, when he was in the full possession of his powers, and when he had already achieved fame.

Suddenly an awful calamity befell him in the death of his wife by accident. One sad day in July, 1861, Mrs. Longfellow's light dress caught fire from a match fallen on the floor. The poet rushed to her aid; but despite all his efforts her injuries were fatal. She died the next morning. Longfellow himself was so severely burned that he was unable to be present at her funeral.

When his wounds healed he was still broken in spirit. To give himself occupation, and to help him bear his sorrow, he translated into English the "Divine Comedy" of Dante. He found the labor of translation restful and consoling, as Bryant had also found it after the death of his wife. In time Longfellow completed his version of the great Italian poem, and it was published in 1867. But while laboring on this long task he had not given up original composition. In 1863 he had sent forth a volume of poems containing the ringing lines on the sinking of the "Cumberland"; and in 1867 another collection in which was included his touching poem on the burial of Hawthorne.

Saw I in the mountains in the heavens,
In the serene sky, the raindrops,
Whispered, "What is that, Nicholas?"
And the good Nicholas answered,
"'T is the heavens of flowers you see there;
All the wild flowers of the forest,
All the lilies of the prairies,
When on earth they fade and perish,
Blossom in the heavens above us,"

Henry W. Longfellow.

May 13, 1888.

During these years also Longfellow was engaged on a
work exactly suited to his powers.  As a poet he was not
primarily a thinker, like Emerson, nor was he chiefly a
musician in verse, like Poe; he was above all a ballad
singer, a teller of stories fit to be said or sung.  Certain
of his friends were in the habit of spending the summer
at the old tavern of Sudbury, and this suggested to the
poet the framework of a book.  He has represented a
group of guests gathered about the fire, and beguiling the
time with story telling.  The first part of these "Tales of a
Wayside Inn" was published in 1863, and two other parts
followed in 1872 and 1873.  Among the tales are some of
Longfellow's best ballads — such as "Paul Revere's Ride,"
"King Robert of Sicily," and "Scanderbeg."

In the spring of 1868 Longfellow went with his daugh-
ters to Europe, and received everywhere an admiring welcome.  In England both Oxford and Cambridge conferred
honorary degrees on him; and the Queen invited him to
dine with her at Windsor Castle.  He spent the winter in
Rome, and came home in 1869.

After his return Longfellow took up and finished his
longest work — "Christus, a Mystery," in which he finally
combined the "Divine Tragedy," the "Golden Legend,"
and the "New England Tragedies."  His liking for the
dramatic form grew in his later years; and the "Masque
of Pandora," which he published in 1875, was actually set
to music and sung on the stage, but with little success.
Afterward he wrote another tragedy — "Judas Macca-
bæus"; and after his death yet another, "Michael Angelo,"
was found almost finished in his desk.  There are fine
passages in all these poems in dialogue; but no one of his
attempts at play-making was received with the popular
approval which greeted his songs and his sonnets.

Two of the longer of his later poems — the " Hanging
of the Crane" (1874) and "Keramos" (1878) — showed
that his hand had not lost its cunning as the poet grew
older; and nothing he had written exceeded in sonorous
rhythm and in lofty sentiment the poem which he read in
1875 at the fiftieth anniversary of his graduation from
Bowdoin, and which he called " Morituri Salutamus "
( " We who are about to die salute you " ).

His poetic gift continued to ripen and to bear mellow
fruit to the end of his life ; and among the lyrics in his
final volumes — " Ultima Thule," published in 1880, and
" In the Harbor," printed after his death in 1882 — were
poems as tender and as delicate in their strength as any
he had written in his youth : the " Chamber over the
Gate," for example, and the very last verses he ever wrote
— the " Bells of San Blas."

It was on March 15, 1882, when Longfellow had just
celebrated his seventy-fifth birthday, that he penned the
final lines of this final poem : —

> Out of the shadows of night
> The world rolls into light.
> It is daybreak everywhere.

The eighteenth was on a Saturday ; and in the afternoon
there came four schoolboys from Boston, who had asked
permission to visit him.   He showed them the view of the
Charles from the window of his study, and with his customary kindness he wrote his autograph in their albums.
That night he was seized with pain ; but he would not dis-
turb the household until the morning.  He lingered a week,
and died on Friday, March 24, 1882.   He was buried the
next Sunday in Mount Auburn Cemetery, "under the
gently falling snow."

Longfellow is the most popular poet yet born in America; and if we can measure popular approval by the widespread sale of his successive volumes, he was probably the most popular poet of the English language in this century. Part of his popularity is due to his healthy mind, his calm spirit, his vigorous sympathy. His thought, though often deep, was never obscure. His lyrics had always a grace that took the ear with delight. They have a singing simplicity, caught, it may be, from the German lyrists, such as Uhland or Heine. This simplicity was the result of rare artistic repression; it was not due to any poverty of intellect.

Like Victor Hugo in France, Longfellow in America was the poet of childhood. And as he understood the children, so he also sympathized with the poor, the toiling, the lowly — not looking down on them, but glorifying their labor, and declaring the necessity of it and the nobility of work. He could make the barest life seem radiant with beauty. He had acquired the culture of all lands, but he understood also the message of his own country. He thought that the best that Europe could bring was none too good for the plain people of America. He was a true American, not only in his stalwart patriotism in the hour of trial, but in his loving acceptance of the doctrine of human equality, and in his belief and trust in his fellow-man.

QUESTIONS. — What was Longfellow's place among the men who formed a remarkable group in New England in the first quarter of the present century?

Speak of Longfellow's family connections; of his boyhood; and of his opportunities for gaining an education.

In what official way was Longfellow's scholarship recognized by two institutions of learning?

In what early works does Longfellow show the influence of two earlier American authors — one a writer in prose, the other in verse?

By what one of his poems did Longfellow win a swift and abiding popularity?

What is the secret of his success in the kind of poems of which the " Skeleton in Armor " is an example?

What events of importance to Longfellow clustered around the year 1843?

Mention the circumstances under which Longfellow came to write the most beautiful tale in verse that had yet been told by any American poet.

How was Longfellow's last prose work characterized by Hawthorne?

How is Longfellow's skill in versification shown in his poems?

What American subjects now furnished Longfellow with the themes of two poems which rivaled in popularity even his story of the Acadian exiles?

What did Longfellow do after the death of his wife?

Discuss Longfellow's dramatic work.

Give the titles of ten of Longfellow's poems not elsewhere referred to in these questions.

Characterize Longfellow as a man and as a poet.

NOTE. — The only complete edition of Longfellow's works is that published by Houghton, Mifflin & Co. (11 vols., $16.50). The Cambridge edition contains all the poems in a single volume ($2). " Evangeline,"· the " Courtship of Miles Standish," " Hiawatha," the " Children's Hour," etc., the " Tales of a Wayside Inn," the " Building of the Ship," etc., can be had as separate numbers of the Riverside Literature series (Houghton, Mifflin & Co., 15 cents).

The best life of Longfellow is that written by his brother, Samuel, and containing abundant extracts from his journal and correspondence (Houghton, Mifflin & Co., 3 vols., $6).

For criticism, see Mr. E. C. Stedman (in " American Poets ") ; Mr. H. E. Scudder (in " Men and Letters ") ; Prof. C. F. Richardson (in his history of " American Literature ") ; Mr. A. Lang (in his " Letters on Literature ") ; Mr. Gannett's " Studies in Longfellow "; and G. W. Curtis (in " Literary and Social Essays ").

## XI  JOHN GREENLEAF WHITTIER

IN the town of Haverhill, Massachusetts, near the
Merrimac River, not far from Salisbury Beach, and in a
house built by his great-great-grandfather more than two
centuries ago, John Greenleaf Whittier was born on
December 17, 1807.  He believed that his ancestors were
Huguenots — and this French Protestant stock is the
ablest and the sturdiest of all the many which have
mingled to make the modern American.  For three generations before him, the family had been connected with
the Society of Friends; and all his life long Whittier

retained not a little of the Quaker simplicity of manner and attire.

The house was surrounded by woods, and "a small brook, noisy enough as it foamed, rippled, and laughed down its rocky falls," by the garden-side.   Then it wound its way to a larger stream, that, "after doing its duty at two or three saw and grist mills" (the clash of which

Whittier's Birthplace

would be heard in still days across the intervening wood-lands), ran into the great river and was borne along to the great sea.   Thus in early boyhood Whittier had a chance to get friendly and familiar with brooks and woods and rocky hills and all the other details of the New England landscape.   He began early to do the chores of the house-hold and also to aid his father in the work of the farm. He helped to care for the oxen and the other beasts of burden, and he came to know the wilder animals which also lived on the farm. His chief companion was a sister, who was six years younger, and who devoted herself to him for half a century.

In his boyhood Whittier had scant instruction, for the district school was open only a few weeks in winter, and its teachers were rarely competent. He had but few books, for there were scarcely thirty in the house, mostly dry disquisitions on theology. The one book he could read and read again until he had it by heart almost was the Bible; and the Bible was always the book which exerted the strongest literary influence upon him.

But when he was fourteen a teacher came who lent him books of travel and opened a new world to him. It was this teacher who brought to the Whittiers one evening a volume of Burns and read aloud some of the poems, after explaining the Scottish dialect. Whittier begged the loan of the book, which contained almost the first rimes he had ever read. It was this volume of Burns which set Whittier to making verses himself, serving both as the motive and the model of his earlier poetic efforts. The Scottish poet, with his homely pictures of a life as bare and as hardy as that of New England then, first revealed to the American poet what poetry really is, and how it might be made out of the actual facts of existence.

That book of Burns's poems had an even stronger influence on Whittier than the odd volume of the "Spectator" which fell into the hands of Franklin had on that American author whose boyhood was most like Whittier's. Franklin was also born in a humble and hard-working family, doing early his share of the labor, and having but a meager education, although always longing for learning. It is true that Irving and Cooper and Bryant did not graduate

from college, but they could have done so had they persevered ; and Emerson and Longfellow and Hawthorne
did get as much of the higher education as was then
possible in America.  But neither Franklin nor Whittier
ever had the chance ; it was as much as they could do in
boyhood to pick up the merest elements of an education.

After he had made the acquaintance of Burns's poems,
Whittier began to scribble rimes of his own on his slate
at school, and in the evening about the family hearth.
One of his boyish quatrains lingered in the memory of an
elder sister : —

> And must I always swing the flail,
> And help to fill the milking pail?
> I wish to go away to school ;
> I do not wish to be a fool.

With practice he began to be bolder, and he wrote verses
on contemporary events and also little ballads.  One of
these, written when he was seventeen, his eldest sister
liked so well that she sent it to the weekly paper of
Newburyport, the *Free Press*, recently started by William
Lloyd Garrison.  She did this without telling her brother,
and no one was more surprised than he when he opened
the paper and found his own verses in the " Poet's Corner."
He was aiding his father to mend a stone wall by the road-
side as the postman passed on horseback and tossed the
paper to the young man.  " His heart stood still a moment
when he saw his own verses.  Such delight as his comes
only once in the lifetime of any aspirant to literary fame.
His father at last called to him to put up the paper and
keep at work."

The editor of the *Free Press* was only three years older
than the poet, although far more mature.  He did more for
the young man than merely print these boyish verses, for

he went to Whittier's father and urged the need of giving the youth a little better education. To do this was not possible then; but two years later, when Whittier was nineteen, an academy was started at Haverhill, and here he attended, even writing a few stanzas to be sung at the opening exercises.

He studied at Haverhill for two terms, earning the little money needed to pay his way by making slippers, by keeping books, and by teaching school. At Haverhill he was able to read the works of many authors hitherto unknown to him, and he also wrote for the local papers much prose and verse. There was even an attempt to get subscribers for a collection of his poems, but it failed, fortunately; and the improving taste of Whittier, when he did publish his first volume, led him to reject most of these early verses.

By the time he was twenty-one he had fitted himself to earn his living by his pen. He went to Boston in 1829 to edit a paper there; and he returned to Haverhill the next year to take charge of the local journal. Then he was at the head of an important weekly at Hartford. In these various positions he acquitted himself well, mastering the questions of the day carefully, and expressing his opinions forcibly and courteously. But his health failed, owing partly perhaps to the exposure and toil of his boyhood on the farm; and in 1832 he gave up journalism for a while and went back to his father's house. He had never been robust, and all his life long he was forced to take care of himself and to husband his strength.

But if the body was weak, the spirit was strong; Whittier had the stout heart which leads a forlorn hope unhesitatingly. Before he was thirty he had made up his mind that it was his duty to do what he could for the relief. of the unfortunate negroes who were held in bondage in the

South.   In 1833 he wrote a pamphlet called "Justice and
Expediency," in which he considered the whole question
of slavery, and declared the necessity of its abolition.
Three years later he became secretary of the Antislavery
Society.   In 1838 he went to Philadelphia to edit the
*Pennsylvania Freeman;* and so boldly did he advocate
the right of the negro to own himself that the printing
office was sacked by a mob and burned.   Then, as more
than once afterward for the same cause, Whittier was in
danger of his life.

Whittier showed physical courage in facing the ruffians
who wished to prevent free speech; but he had revealed
the higher moral courage in casting in his lot with the
little band of abolitionists.   He had looked forward to
political preferment, as well he might, when many another
journalist was stepping from the newspaper desk into
public life.   When he became one of the very small mi-
nority who denounced slavery, he gave up all chance of
office.   He also had literary ambition, but so strong was
the power of the slave owners then, and so intolerant were
they, that most editors and publishers were sorely intimi-
dated, and declined to print any attack on slavery, and
even the other writings of an author who was known
as an abolitionist.   Thus Whittier, in identifying himself
with the antislavery movement, thought that he was giving up his literary future also.   He made his decision
promptly, and he never regretted it.   Indeed, in later life
he said to a boy of fifteen to whom he was giving counsel,
" My lad, if thou wouldst win success, join thyself to some
unpopular but noble cause."

By constant practice he had acquired ease in composition; but as his hand gained strength his taste also improved, and little of this earlier writing satisfied him for

long. A miscellany of prose and verse called "Legends of New England," published in 1831, was his first book. It contained a selection of the best of the poems and the essays he had printed here and there in periodicals. In later life he thought so slightly of this volume that none of the essays, and only two of the poems, were republished in the revised edition of his works. Immature as was this youthful verse, scarcely any American had then written better. Bryant's first volume, and Poe's, had been published several years before ; but Longfellow's earliest book of poems, "Voices of the Night," did not appear until 1839, to be followed in 1847 by the first collection of Emerson's poems.

Other poems, which Whittier discarded in later life, were published in the next few years. The most vigorous of the verses he wrote at this time were inspired by his hatred of slavery. From the day he threw himself into the abolition movement, his verse had a loftier note and a more resonant tone. With him poetry was then no longer a mere amusement or accomplishment; it had become a weapon for use in the good fight.

In these antislavery poems there is a noble passion and a righteous anger. They were calls to a battle with evil ; and the best of them rang out like blasts of a bugle. One collection of these antislavery verses was published in 1837, and a second, called "Voices of Freedom," appeared in 1849. When we compare either of these volumes with Longfellow's "Poems on Slavery" (printed in 1842, midway between them), we see how much sturdier Whittier's stanzas are, and how much more his heart is in the cause than Longfellow's. It is Longfellow who writes with Quaker-like gentleness, and it is Whittier who fiercely sounds the trumpet of battle.

In other ways also is the contrast between Longfellow and Whittier interesting and instructive. Both were New Englanders, and both hated slavery. Longfellow was the most literary of all our poets, and Whittier was perhaps the least. By consummate art Longfellow sometimes achieved simplicity, but he never could attain the homely directness natural to Whittier. Longfellow's chief service to our literature was in showing how it was possible to get

Whittier's Residence, Amesbury, Mass.

the best that Europe and the storied past could give, and yet to remain an American of the present. Whittier dealt almost wholly with the facts of American life, with the legends and the thoughts, with the landscape and the people of New England. Where Longfellow was cosmopolitan, Whittier was less than national even, he was sectional; and he was therefore too local in his themes and in his manner to win popularity in England as Longfellow did. Here in the United States, however, where the influence of New England is widespread and abiding, Whittier came at last to have a popularity second only to Longfellow's, and due largely to the fact that he, more than any other, was the representative poet of New England.

Whittier was the only one of the leading American poets who never crossed the Atlantic. Not only did he never go to Europe, he never went south of the Potomac or west of the Alleghanies. When the farm at Haverhill was sold in 1836, part of the price was used to buy a small place at Amesbury; and that house was Whittier's home for more than half a century. After his return from Philadelphia, in 1839, he was rarely absent from Amesbury for more than a month or two at a time, although he did once reside the better part of a year in Lowell. He made visits to Boston often and sometimes even to New York; and frequently he spent his summers elsewhere; but until his death his home was the little house at Amesbury.

Though his abolition sentiments were boldly insisted upon in most of his writings, they did not prevent the steady rise of his poetic reputation even among those who were not of his way of thinking. With the publication in 1843 of "Lays of My Home," Whittier made sure his place among American poets. In this volume are some of the best of his ballads,—"Cassandra Southwick," for one—and as a writer of ballads Longfellow only, among all the American poets, was Whittier's superior.

He had the gift of story-telling in verse. He did not strain his invention to devise a strange plot; he took an old legend or a tale of real life, and he set it forth in rime simply and easily. He had the touch of genius which transfigures common things. He sang of what he knew, the fields where he played as a boy, the river and the hills he had gazed on in childhood, the men and women who had grown up about him, the thoughts and the sentiments he and they had inherited together. Even the unpromising proper names of New England become melodious in his hands.

As the years passed, Whittier's powers ripened and the level of his work was raised ; but the quality of the poems included in "Songs of Labor," published in 1850, and in "Home Ballads," published in 1860, is the quality of the collection published in 1843. Among the verse written during these seventeen years are the "Angels of Buena Vista" ; "Maud Muller" (perhaps the most popular of all his briefer poems), "Ichabod " (perhaps the loftiest of all laments over fallen greatness) ; the "Barefoot Boy" ; " Skipper Ireson's Ride " (one of his most characteristic New England ballads) ; and the tribute to Robert Burns. The poet of New England was always swift to declare his indebtedness to the poet of Scotland and to proclaim his abiding regard for the poems which had first shown him what poetry was.

During these years of the antislavery struggle not only was Whittier's reputation as a poet growing steadily, but the people of the North and of the West were as steadily coming over to his side. Of course we cannot exactly measure the influence of a lyric, but it may be almost irresistible. He was a wise man who was willing to let others make the laws of a people if only he could make their songs. Law is but the condensation of public opinion ; and when the ringing stanzas of the antislavery bards and the speeches of the antislavery orators had awakened the conscience of the free states, the end of the evil was nigh. Slavery made a hard fight for its life ; but

it was slavery itself that Whittier hated, and not the
slave owners; and there is no bitterness or rancor in the
poems published in 1863 and called "In War Time." Even
in his most martial lines there is a Quaker suavity; and
of these ballads of the battle years the best known is
"Barbara Frietchie," a testimony to the old flag, not a
diatribe against those who were then attacking it, and
founded on a misapprehension of the facts.

After the final triumph of the cause for which he had
battled long and bravely, Whittier turned again to peaceful
themes.   With the spread of his opinions among the
people, his poetry had also become more popular; but no
single book of his had ever a widespread and immediate
success until "Snow-Bound" appeared in 1866.   This
poem of New England was seen at once to be worthy
of comparison with the "Deserted Village" and with
the "Cotter's Saturday Night," with more of the real
flavor of the soil than Goldsmith's lines, and with less
breadth, but no less elevation, than Burns's.   It was
received by the reading public as no other poem since
Longfellow's "Evangeline" and "Hiawatha."   It was so
profitable that for the first time in his life — and he was
then nearly sixty — Whittier was placed above want.

Only less successful was the "Tent on the Beach,"
printed the next year, and followed in twelve months by
"Among the Hills."   Thereafter his position was secure.
He had taken his place as one of the poets of America,
beside Emerson and Longfellow, beside Lowell and
Holmes; and perhaps he was nearer than any of the
others to the hearts of New Englanders and of the
Westerners whose fathers had gone out from New England.   He has been called a Quaker Burns; he might
better be called the Burns of New England; and as Burns

# Sweet Fern.

The subtle power the perfume found
    Nor seer nor sibyl vainly learned
On Grecian shrine or Aztec mound
    No cender idly burned.

That power the hoary wizard knew
    The dervish in his frenzied dance,
The Pythian priestess swooning through
    The wonder-land of trance.

And Nature holds in wood & field
    Her thousand sun-lit censers still;
To spells of flower & shrub we yield
    Against or with our will.

I climbed a hill-path strange & new,
    With slow feet, pausing at each turn.
A sudden waft of west wind blew
    The breath of this sweet fern.

That fragrance from my vision swept
    The alien landscape; in its stead
Up fairer hills of youth I stepped
    As light of heart as tread.

wrote for Scotland rather than for the whole of Great
Britain, so Whittier wrote for New England rather than
for the whole of the United States. It was the scenery
of New England he loved best to paint in his ballads;
it was the sentiments of New England he voiced in his
lyrics; it was his steadfast faith in New England that
gave strength to all he wrote.

During the later years of his life Whittier wrote as the
mood came, and he gathered his scattered verses into
volumes from time to time — "Ballads of New England,"
for example, in 1870; "Mabel Martin," in 1874; the
"King's Missive," in 1881. While no one of these collections repeated the impression made by "Snow-Bound," they
strengthened his hold on the hearts of the people. No
doubt his old age was made happier by the honor in which
he was held. Though his health was not good, he came
of sturdy stock, and he outlived the most of his fellow-
poets of New England. He saw Longfellow go first, and
then Emerson, and finally Lowell, his comrade in the antislavery struggle. Long past the allotted three-score years
and ten, he printed a final volume of his poems in 1892,
under the significant title "At Sundown." At last, early in
the fall of 1892, he had a slight paralytic shock, and he died
at dawn on September 7, being then in his eighty-fifth year.

It is as a poet that Whittier is held most in honor, but
he was also a writer of prose; and in the final collected
edition of his works published four years before his death
his prose writings fill three of the seven volumes. Of
these prose writings the most important is an attempt to
reconstruct (in the form of a diary) the life of the first
settlers; it is called "Margaret Smith's Journal in the
Province of Massachusetts Bay, 1678–79," and it was first
published in 1849. As the poet himself said, "Its merit

consists mainly in the fact that it presents a tolerably life-
like picture of the past, and introduces us familiarly to the
hearts and homes of New England in the seventeenth
century." The poet also preserved in these three volumes
what seemed to him best worth keeping of all his earlier
tales and sketches and of his later literary criticisms and
personal tributes.

He revised at the same time the more important of his
antislavery tracts and articles. As slavery has been abol-
ished forever in this country, the interest of these polemic
writings is now mainly historical; they show us how the
men felt and thought who were in the thick of the fight
for freedom. It is the hard fate of nearly all writing
done to aid a cause that it is killed by its own success.
Just as soon as the result is attained the articles which
helped to bring about the result cease to reward reading.
From this hard fate much of Whittier's antislavery and
war poetry is saved by its own intrinsic beauty — a beauty
lacking in his prose, however. The same neglect has also
befallen not a little of the vigorous writing of Benjamin
Franklin.

Unlike as Whittier and Franklin were in many respects,
they were alike in others. Both of them had the sympathy with the lowly which comes of early experience.
Both learned a handicraft, for as a boy Franklin set type
and worked a printing press, and Whittier had learnt the
trade of slipper-making. To both of them literature was
a means, rather than an end in itself. Verse to Whittier, and prose to Franklin, was a weapon to be used in
the good fight. In Whittier's verse, as in Franklin's
prose, there was the same pithy directness which made
their words go home to the hearts of the plain people
whom they both understood and represented.

In the fortunate absence of any class distinctions in this country, both Franklin and Whittier were able to develop at will, expanding freely as occasion served, and educating themselves into harmony with broader opportunities. To Franklin was given the larger life and the greater range of usefulness ; but Whittier always did with all his might the duty that lay before him.

While Whittier was practical, as becomes a New Englander, he had not the excessive common sense which characterizes Franklin, and he lacked also Franklin's abundant humor. So also his morality was of finer fiber than Franklin's. He was not content, as Franklin was, with showing that honesty is the best policy, and that in the long run vice does not pay ; he scourged evil with the wrath of a Hebrew prophet. His views of life were Hebraic rather than Hellenic, for he sought duty, as the Jews did, rather than beauty, as did the Greeks. No one of his poems was written for its own sake, with the exception only of a few of his ballads. They were nearly all intended to further a cause he held dear, or to teach a lesson he thought needful.

For the most part his art was unconscious ; he sang because he was a born poet. He was not an artist in verse as Longfellow was ; and he was often as careless in rime and as rugged in rhythm as was Emerson. Yet to some of his stanzas there is a lyric lilt that sings itself into the memory ; and the best of his ballads have an easy grace of movement. He knew his own deficiencies of training, and he was quick to take advice from those whom he thought better equipped than himself. In this as in all things else he was modest. How modest he really was is perhaps best shown in certain quatrains of the poem he called " My Triumph " : —

O living friends who love me!
O dear ones gone above me!
Careless of other fame,
I leave to you my name.

Hide it from idle praises,
Save it from evil phrases;
Why, when dear lips that spake it
Are dumb, should strangers wake it?

Let the thick curtain fall;
I better know than all
How little I have gained,
How vast the unattained.

Sweeter than any sung
My songs that found no tongue;
Nobler than any fact
My wish that failed of act.

Others shall sing the song,
Others shall right the wrong —
Finish what I begin —
And all I fail of win.


QUESTIONS. — How in his boyhood did Whittier learn to love Nature?

With what kinds of books did he first become acquainted?

Compare his educational advantages with those of other American men of letters.

Tell how he made the acquaintance of the leading antislavery agitator of his day, and in what way the connection was beneficial to him.

What efforts and sacrifices did Whittier make in order to be of service to the cause to which he devoted himself?

Trace the growth of Whittier's literary skill during the twenty years of this period in his life.

Contrast the representative New England poet with the representative American poet.

Characterize the work in three collections of Whittier's poems published between 1843 and 1860.

Discuss Whittier's service in the cause which his book "In War Time " was designed to further.

Compare with the most famous works of Burns and Goldsmith the poem by which Whittier won a degree of literary and financial success surpassing anything which he had known hitherto.

What is the general character of Whittier's later poems?

What can you say of Whittier's reputation as a writer in prose?

Compare Whittier and Franklin.

Make an estimate of Whittier's art.

NOTE. — The only complete edition of Whittier's works is that published by Houghton, Mifflin & Co. (7 vols., $10.50). The Cambridge edition contains all the poems in a single volume ($2). "Snow-Bound," " Mabel Martin," etc., the " Tent on the Beach," etc., can be had as separate numbers of the Riverside Literature series (Houghton, Mifflin & Co., 15 cents).

The authoritative biography is that of Mr. S. T. Pickard (Houghton, Mifflin & Co., 2 vols., $3).

For criticism, see Lowell's " Fable for Critics"; Mr. E. C. Stedman (in his " American Poets "); Prof. C. F. Richardson (in his history of " American Literature "); Prof. Barrett Wendell (in his " Stelligeri "); Mrs. Fields (in a volume of Harper's Black and White series); and Prof. George E. Woodberry (in *Atlantic Monthly*, November, 1892).

## XII   EDGAR   ALLAN   POE

With scarcely an exception the chief authors of America have lived out their allotted threescore years and ten; and their long lives have been happy; and at last they have died surrounded by friends and held in high honor by their fellow-countrymen.  Franklin and Irving, Bryant and Emerson, Longfellow and Lowell, Holmes and Whittier, all survived to a ripe old age.  James Fenimore Cooper, although often harassed by petty squabbles due to his own touchiness of temper, was completely happy at his own fireside; and Nathaniel Hawthorne, although so much of a recluse by nature as to seem to some almost a mis-anthrope, was quite as fortunate in his home life as Cooper was.

The single exception to this remarkable record of pros-perous and honorable longevity is Edgar Allan Poe, who died young and alone and poor and in ill repute. And yet in the eyes of foreigners he is the most gifted of all the authors of America; he is the one to whom the critics of Europe would most readily accord the full title of genius. At the end of this nineteenth century Poe is the sole man of letters born in the United States whose writings are read eagerly in Great Britain and in France, in Germany, in Italy, and in Spain, where Franklin is now but a name and where the fame of James Fenimore Cooper, once as widely spread, is now slowly fading away.

And in yet another respect is Poe unlike the other American authors of this century; they may be divided into two geographical groups — Irving, Cooper, and Bry-ant in New York; and Emerson, Longfellow, Hawthorne, Whittier, Holmes, and Lowell in New England. Poe was neither a New Yorker nor a New Englander; he was a Southerner both by temperament and by descent.

That he chanced to be born in Boston — on January 19, 1809 — was an accident due to the fact that his parents happened to be attached to a theatrical company then performing there. His father was a son of David Poe, a revolutionary patriot of Baltimore. His mother was an actress of much skill and of high character. After the death of his father his mother joined the company in Richmond; and there she died also, before Edgar was three years old.

He was a beautiful and precocious child; and the wife of a Richmond merchant named Allan received him into the family. The boy was thereafter called Edgar Allan Poe. His parents had been very poor; and he was now on the footing of an adopted son in the household of a wealthy and liberal man. He was sent to school, and at the age of six he could read and draw and dance. "It is related also," says a biographer, "that Mr. Allan taught the boy to stand up in a chair at dessert and pledge the health of the company, which he did with roguish grace," and which may have implanted in him then the seeds of a fatal desire for strong drink.

In 1815 the Allans went to England and Edgar was put to school in the outskirts of London, where he took part in outdoor sports and studied Latin and French. Five years later, when the boy was eleven, the family returned to Richmond and he was again sent to a good school. He began to write verses; he led in the school debates and in the school athletics; but he made no intimate friends. Even as a boy he seems to have been self-willed, "proud of his powers and fond of their successful display." One of his schoolboy feats at the age of sixteen was to swim from Richmond to Warwick, a distance of five or six miles. After he left school he studied for a while under excellent tutors; and then at the age of seventeen he matriculated at the University of Virginia, where he remained a little longer than a year.

His scholarship was praised while he was there, and he was on good terms with the authorities. But his character was declaring itself; he was sometimes solitary and reserved; and sometimes he drank to excess and played cards beyond his means. At the close of the session Mr. Allan refused to pay these gambling debts and took Poe away from the university, giving him a desk in the counting room at Richmond. Perhaps Poe felt himself unfitted for business, and perhaps its restraints were irksome. At all events he soon broke away finally.

In May, 1827 — being again in Boston — he enlisted in the United States Army, under the name of Edgar A. Perry, giving his age as twenty-two (when he was really only eighteen). He served in the artillery for nearly two years, first in the harbor of Boston, then at Fort Moultrie near Charleston, and finally at Fortress Monroe. He seems to have discharged his duties to the satisfaction of his officers, and he was even promoted to be Sergeant Major. After the death of Mrs. Allan, he was reconciled with her husband, who procured Edgar's honorable discharge from the army and afterwards got him an appointment as a cadet at West Point.

He entered the Military Academy in July, 1830, being then twenty-one but declaring himself to be only nineteen. He was shy and reserved with his fellow-cadets. His French was fluent and he had an aptitude for mathematics, so that the hard work of the education the government gives its officers was easy for him. But he showed a gross contempt for his military duties ; and probably the service was not alluring to him.

Shortly after he entered West Point Mr. Allan married again ; and Poe knew that he could no longer hope to inherit any portion of that gentleman's fortune. Having the ample confidence of youthful ability, he resolved to face the world for himself. By absence from roll call and guard duty and by disobedience to the orders of the officer of the day, he made certain his dismissal after trial by court-martial. And in March, 1831, being then twenty-two years old, he left West Point to begin the battle of life alone.

He had arranged with his fellow-cadets to subscribe for a volume of his poetry. Already in Boston in 1827 he had published a thin little book containing "Tamerlane and Other Poems," not more immature than juvenile verses usually are. Two years later in Baltimore he had published what was really an enlargement of this first venture, "Al Aaraaf, Tamerlane, and Minor Poems." The collection published in New York in 1831 contained revised versions of these earlier metrical essays, with the addition of his later verses ; it was called simply "Poems " and it was dedicated to the cadets of the Military Academy. Although Poe probably made a little money by the subscriptions to this book, it failed to make any deep impression on the public.

The next four years were for Poe a period of hard struggle and bitter poverty. He began to write short stories ; and one of these, a tale of striking vigor and novelty, the "MS. found in a Bottle," won him a hundred-dollar prize offered by a newspaper for the best brief fiction sent to it. But he could not find a publisher willing to issue the volume of tales of which this was one. There were times when he was in want of the absolute necessities of life — when he was insufficiently clothed and when he lacked food itself. But he had friends who encouraged him and helped him in many ways.

At last, in 1835, one of these friends got him the post of assistant editor of the *Southern Literary Messenger*, a new monthly review just started in Richmond. For a position of this character he immediately showed himself to be remarkably well fitted ; and under his control the *Messenger* promptly became the leading literary periodical of the South. Poe printed in it his own poems and short stories, and thus began to make himself known as an imaginative writer of strange originality and power. As a critic also he revealed unexpected strength ; he had fixed principles of literary art and he applied these principles fairly and fearlessly to the writings of the time. Indeed, in this earlier part of Poe's career as an author he was known rather as a critic than as a poet or as a romancer.

Having an assured income from the *Southern Literary Messenger* sufficient for his support, he married his cousin, Virginia Clemm. This was in May, 1836, and he was then twenty-seven years old ; the bride was barely fourteen. He made a tender and a devoted husband. The future now seemed bright before him : he had a loving wife and loyal friends ; he had a comfortable home and congenial work ; he was rapidly making himself known as an author from whom much might be expected. Then suddenly he let his fortune slip through his hands ; he yielded again to the temptation of drink ; and a few months after his marriage he lost his place on the *Messenger*.

The record of the thirteen remaining years of Poe's life is one long sequence of similar opportunities wasted in like manner. He had many friends always willing to help him along ; and his ability as an editor was indisputable. But whatever the position he undertook to fill, and however firmly he might set about his duties, the fatal weakness always reappeared sooner or later. As the years passed over him, the temptation became more and more difficult to resist. When he was sober he was hard working, faithful to his duties, and courteous to all. But toward the end of his life the periods of sobriety were briefer, as his will was enfeebled by constant yielding.

After leaving Richmond Poe published, in 1838, the "Narrative of Arthur Gordon Pym," a fictitious story of Antarctic adventure, made real by the constant description of unimportant detail, somewhat in the manner of "Robinson Crusoe."

In 1840 he succeeded in finding a publisher for the "Tales of the Grotesque and the Arabesque," the most original collection of short stories written by any American author, with the sole exception of the volume of "Twice-Told Tales" which Hawthorne had sent forth from his obscurity three years before. It is to be recorded that Poe was one of the first to recognize the genius of Hawthorne. The story-teller of the South swiftly discovered in the romancer of the North certain of the rare qualities which he knew himself to possess and which he ardently admired — invention, and imagination, and a mastery of the weird and the mysterious.

While there was in the "Tales of the Grotesque and the Arabesque" a certain Southern affluence and luxuriance, and in the "Twice-Told Tales" a certain Northern severity and restraint, both authors showed in these books that they had not only the native gift of story-telling but also that they had acquired the art of narrative. Any tale of theirs, twice-told, or grotesque and arabesque, had always unity of conception, adroit perspective, and just proportion.

Perhaps the knowledge that Hawthorne had had a post in the Boston customhouse suggested to Poe that he should also try to secure a place in the government service. This was during his six years' residence in Philadelphia after he left Richmond. He failed to get the appointment he sought. But fortune favored him again and again, and he had other places. He acted as editor of one magazine after another, always increasing its circulation by his skill and his activity, and always losing his position at last either because he quarreled with the proprietor or because he lapsed again into his old habits and then neglected his duties. The fidelity with which Poe did his allotted work and the courtesy he showed toward

# The Rationale of Verse. *

## 'By Edgar A. Poe.

The word "Verse" is here used not in its strict or primitive sense, but as the term most convenient for expressing generally and without pedantry all that is involved in the consideration of rhythm, rhyme, metre, and versification.

There is, perhaps, no topic in polite literature which has been more pertinaciously discussed, and there is certainly not one about which so much inaccuracy, confusion, misconception, misrepresentation, mystification, and downright ignorance on all sides, can be fairly said to exist. Were the topic really difficult, or did it lie, even, in the cloud-land of metaphysics, where the doubt-vapors may be made to assume any and every shape at the will or at the fancy of the gazer, we should have less reason to wonder at all this con-tradiction and perplexity; but in fact the subject is exceedingly simp-

be; one tenth of it, possibly, may be called ethical; nine tenths, however, appertain to the mathematics; and the whole is included within the limits of the commonest common sense.

"But, if this is the case, how," it will be asked, "can so much misunderstanding have arisen? Is it conceivable that a thousand profound scholars, investigating so very simple a matter for centuries, have not been able to place it in the fullest light, at least, of which it is susceptible?" These queries, I confess, are not easily answered:—at all events, a satisfactory reply to them might cost more trouble than would, if properly considered, the whole vexata questio to which they have reference. Nevertheless, there is little difficulty or danger in suggesting that the "thousand profound scholars" may have builded

*Some passages of this article appeared, about four years ago, in "The Pioneer," a monthly Magazine published by J. R. Lowell and R. Carter. Although an excellent work it had a very limited circulation.

163

his employers during the periods when he retained his self-control were in marked contrast with his characteristics when he had yielded to temptation, for then he was neglectful, touchy, and suspicious.

As a writer his reputation steadily rose during his stay in Philadelphia. In 1841 he published in a magazine the first detective story ever written, the "Murders in the Rue Morgue"; and two years later he won another hundred-dollar prize with a second tale of the same type, the "Gold Bug." Two other stories of hidden secrets skillfully unraveled are his "Mystery of Marie Roget" and the "Purloined Letter." Just as Washington Irving had written the first American local short story in "Rip Van Winkle," and just as James Fenimore Cooper had written the first sea tale in the "Pilot," so Poe in like manner invented the detective story. He has had numberless imitators in this department of fiction; he has had no real rivals. In ingenuity, in variety, in plausibility, in sustained interest and in vigorous logic, the "Murders in the Rue Morgue" and the "Gold Bug" are unsurpassable masterpieces.

After a stay of six years in Philadelphia Poe moved in 1844 to New York, where his residence was for the few remaining years of his life. He had long cherished the hope of starting a monthly magazine of his own, but the project never came to anything, although it always remained the center of Poe's aspirations. He found editorial positions first on one and then on another literary journal in New York, breaking off his connection with them suddenly as was his custom.

His criticisms of his contemporaries were now far sharper than they had been when he first wrote; and they were less honest. As a critic Poe's influence had hitherto been excellent in the main, for he had a better equipment

and a keener insight than any other newspaper reviewer of
the time ; and he had lofty ideals of literary art.   But as
he grew older his opinions seem to have narrowed.   He
had no reverence for Homer or Shakspere or Milton ; he
regarded Keats and Shelley and Coleridge "and a few
others of like expression . . . as the *sole* poets."

Having these one-sided views, he was often violent and
intolerant in setting them forth.   And he allowed his liking
for the person of an author to influence his published opinion of that author's works.   He praised his friends unduly ;
and he was bitter in his attack on those whom he held to
be his enemies.   Even the gentle Longfellow was unfairly
held up to scorn as a poet who pilfered from many predecessors.   One writer whose works he criticised sharply,
retorted with an attack so personal that Poe brought suit
for libel and recovered damages.

Yet at this time Poe's own reputation as a poet had just
been established firmly by the publication of the "Raven "
— perhaps the most widely known poem written by any
American to this day.   It appeared in a magazine early
in 1845 and was instantly copied into the leading newspapers of the United States.   It achieved an immediate
popularity, which continues undiminished to the present
time.   Its reception was so cordial that toward the close
of the year Poe gathered up his other verses, revising
them scrupulously as was his wont, and sent forth a volume called the "Raven and Other Poems."   Hitherto
Poe had been known to the public as a critic chiefly,
and also as a writer of short stories ; thereafter he was
accepted as a poet.

In the preface to this collection of his verses, Poe
declared that poetry had been to him " not a purpose, but a
passion."   By long study he had made himself a master of

the technic of verse, and he combined with extraordinary skill all the effects to be derived from lilting rhythm, intricate rime, artful repetition, and an aptly chosen refrain. He bent words to his bidding, and he made his verse so melodious that it had almost the charm of music.

That his scheme of poetry was highly artificial, that the themes of his poems were vague and insubstantial, and that his stanzas do not stimulate thought — these things may be admitted without disadvantage. What the reader does find in Poe's poetry is the suggestion of departed but imperishable beauty, and the lingering grace and fascination of haunting melancholy. His verses throb with an inexpressible magic and glow with intangible fantasy. His poems have no other purpose; they convey no moral; they echo no call to duty; they celebrate beauty only — beauty immaterial and evanescent; they are their own excuse for being.

In 1846 he moved to a tiny little cottage at Fordham in the outskirts of New York. His wife was dying, and they were in bitter want. He lacked even bedclothes to wrap up the enfeebled woman he loved, and she lay in bed covered with his overcoat. Toward the end of the year a public appeal was made in the newspapers, stating that the family of the poet needed immediate help; and as a result, their necessities were promptly relieved. Poe's "natural pride impelled him to shrink from public charity even at the cost of truth in denying those necessities which were but too real." His wife sank lower and lower day by day, and early in 1847 she died. Poe himself was also ill; and again a subscription on his behalf was taken up in New York.

For a while he lived in retirement, slowly regaining his strength. It was about this time that he wrote the " Bells," one of the most sonorously melodious of his poems, second in popularity only to the "Raven." He also elaborated a pseudo-scientific rhapsody, which he called "Eureka." Before publishing this he delivered part of it as a lecture. He had appeared on the lecture platform more than once already in Philadelphia and in Boston. He was a picturesque and striking speaker; and it is not easy to see

Poe's Cottage, Fordham, N.Y.

why he did not earlier turn his attention to lecturing as a means of pushing his fortunes.

Even before the death of his wife he seems to have allowed himself to be flattered by foolish women, whose now forgotten verses he belauded extravagantly. To one or another of these he went for sympathy, although appar-

ently unable to decide definitely which of them he preferred. He was even engaged to be married to a lady in
Providence, who had to break off the match because he did
not keep his word to her to give up drink. Then he proposed to a lady in Richmond and, so it seems, was accepted.

Toward the end of September, two years after his wife's
death, he left Richmond to arrange for his final removal
from New York. Four or five days later he was found in
Baltimore in the last stages of delirium. He was admitted
to a hospital, and there, on Sunday, October 9, 1849, he
died. His relatives took charge of his funeral and he was
buried the next day.

Thus came to an untimely end the unfortunate genius
who was born in the same year as Oliver Wendell Holmes,
and who died miserably forty years and more before the
close of Holmes's dignified and honorable career. He
had great gifts, perhaps greater than those of any other
American poet, but he knew not how to husband them.
He had many chances, but he threw them away, one by
one. Fortune favored him again and again, but he made
shipwreck of his fate. He won many friends to no purpose, for their unwearied efforts were unavailing to save
him from the consequences of his own weakness of will.
His misfortunes were due to his own failings ; and if he
was unhappy, it was entirely his own fault. He was, as
Lowell said in Poe's lifetime, " wholly lacking in that ele-
ment of manhood which for want of a better name we
call *character;* it is something quite distinct from genius
— though all great geniuses are endowed with it."

QUESTIONS. — Enlarge upon two respects in which Poe is strikingly
unlike the other great American writers of the nineteenth century.

Trace his career to his expulsion from West Point.

Compare Poe's literary ability, as it was revealed by his first important volume, with that of Hawthorne, as this was revealed in the latter's
corresponding work.

Discuss Poe's success in a line of fiction in which he was the
pioneer.

What changes in Poe's disposition and manner began to be evident
after his removal to what was to be his home for the few remaining
years of his life?

What characteristics of Poe's genius at about the same time opened
for him a new literary career?

What were the chief events of the last three years of Poe's life?

How does Lowell's estimate of Poe's character agree with your own?

NOTE. — The only complete edition of Poe's works is that of Mr. Stedman and
Mr. Woodberry (Stone & Kimball, Chicago, 10 vols. at $1.50). Single volume
editions of "Poems" and of the "Tales" are imperfect and not to be recommended.

The best biography is Mr. Woodberry's in the American Men of Letters series
(Houghton, Mifflin & Co., Boston, $1.25). A condensation of this memoir is to be
found in the first volume of the complete edition.

The best criticism of Poe is in Mr. Woodberry's biography, in Mr. Stedman's
"American Poets," and in the introductions to the several divisions of their com-
plete edition. Note also the characterization of Poe in Lowell's "Fable for
Critics"; in Prof. Richardson's history of "American Literature"; in Mr.
T. W. Higginson's "Short Studies of American Authors"; and in Mr. A. Lang's
preface to his edition of Poe's poems. An essay on the short story in Mr. Brander
Matthews's "Pen and Ink" contains a comparison of Poe and Hawthorne as
writers of tales.

## XIII  OLIVER WENDELL HOLMES

OLIVER WENDELL HOLMES was born in Cambridge,
Massachusetts, on August 29, 1809.  During the Revolution his grandfather had served as a surgeon with the
Continental troops; and his father was the author of the
"Annals of America," almost the first attempt at a docu-
mentary history of this country.  He grew to boyhood in
Cambridge, often playing under the Washington elm.  He
was sent to Phillips Academy, Andover; and it was while
he was a schoolboy there that he translated the first book
of Vergil's "Æneid" into heroic couplets — the meter used

by Pope in his version of Homer's "Iliad." Then he went to Harvard College, where he was graduated in 1829, eight years after Emerson and nine years before Lowell. He wrote prose and verse while he was at Harvard, contributing freely to the college paper; and he delivered the poem at commencement.

Settling down in his native town he began to study law, but his heart was not in his task, and he sought relief in writing verse, mostly comic. That he could be serious upon occasion was shown swiftly the year after his graduation, when it was proposed to break up the frigate "Constitution" — "Old Ironsides" — the victor in the splendid fight with the British ship "Guerrière" in the war of 1812. With the hot indignation of youth against what seemed to him an insult and an outrage upon a national glory, Holmes wrote the fiery lines beginning : —

> Ay, tear her tattered ensign down,
>   Long has it waved on high, -
> And many an eye has danced to see
>   That banner in the sky ; -
> Beneath it rung the battle shout,
>   And burst the cannon's roar ; -
> The meteor of the ocean air
>   Shall sweep the clouds no more. -

This lyric appeal to patriotic feeling was first published in the *Boston Advertiser;* it was copied all over the country ; it was quoted in speeches ; it was printed on handbills ; and it saved the ship for half a century. "Old Ironsides" was taken to the new Charlestown navy yard, and a few years later she was thoroughly repaired. Even when the day of wooden war ships was past forever, the "Constitution" did not go out of commission for the last time until about fifty years after Holmes had penned his stirring lines.

Apparently the law did not tempt Holmes to persever-ance; and before he had been out of college two years he abandoned it finally, to take up the study of medicine — his grandfather's profession. Although he had already written much, and was helping to edit a miscellany, he seems never to have thought of authorship as his calling.

Holmes's Birthplace, Cambridge. Mass.

Having made his choice of a profession, Holmes devoted himself to it — at first in Boston, and then in Europe; making the voyage chiefly that he might study medicine in Paris, where the best instruction was to be obtained at that time. "I was in Europe," he wrote half a century later, "about two years and a half, from April, 1833, to October, 1835. I sailed in the packet ship 'Philadelphia' from New York to Portsmouth, where we arrived after a passage of twenty-four days. . . . I then crossed the

Channel to Havre, from which I went to Paris. In the spring and summer of 1834 I made my principal visit to England and Scotland. There were other excursions to the Rhine and to Holland, to Switzerland and to Italy. . . . I returned in the packet-ship 'Utica,' sailing from Havre, and reaching New York after a passage of forty-two days."

He received the degree of Doctor of Medicine in 1836, being then twenty-seven years old ; and in that year he also published his first volume of poems. Nothing of Dr. Holmes's has been more popular than the "Last Leaf" contained in this early collection, and none has more richly deserved to please by its rhythmic beauty, and by its exquisite blending of humor and pathos, so sympathetically intertwined that we feel the lonely sadness of the old man even while we are smiling at his quaintness so delicately portrayed.    Dr. Holmes was like Bryant (who composed "Thanatopsis" and the "Lines to a Waterfowl" long before he was twenty) in that he early attained his full development as a poet. Although both of them wrote many verses in later life, nothing of theirs excelled these poems of their youth.    In their maturity they did not fall off, but neither did they deepen or broaden ; and "Thanatopsis" on the one side, and the "Last Leaf" on the other, are as strong and characteristic as anything either poet was ever to write throughout all his long life.    What Bryant was, what Holmes was, in his first volume of poems, each was to the end of his career.

To neither of them was literature a livelihood.    Bryant was first a lawyer and then a journalist.    Holmes was first a practicing physician and then a teacher of medicine. He won three prizes for dissertations on medical themes, and these essays were published together in 1838.    In 1839 he was appointed professor of anatomy and physiology at Dartmouth and the next year he married Miss Amelia Lee Jackson. Shortly afterward he resigned the professorship at Dartmouth and resumed practice in Boston. He worked hard at his profession, and he contributed freely to its literature — publishing, for example, in 1842 his trenchant discussion of "Homeopathy and its Kindred Delusions." Then, in 1847, he went back to Harvard, having been appointed professor of anatomy and physiology — a position which he was to hold with great distinction for thirty-five years.

The most of the prose which Dr. Holmes wrote at this period of his life was upon medical topics ; and whenever he had anything to say upon other than professional subjects he generally said it in verse. Although he was for a while a frequent lecturer in the lyceums of New England, following in the footsteps of Emerson, his literary reputation until he was nearly fifty was due almost wholly to his poems. This reputation was highest in Massachusetts, and he was the bard of Boston especially, being called upon whenever the three-hilled city needed a copy of verses for an occasion of public interest, a dinner, or a funeral, or the visit of a distinguished foreigner. He always acquitted himself acceptably and often brilliantly ; and he rarely refused to provide the few lines of rime appropriate to the event. As he himself humorously put it in one of his later occasional poems : —

> I'm a florist in verse, and what *would* people say
> If I came to a banquet without my bouquet ?

Then, when Holmes was forty-eight years old, an age at which most men have stiffened themselves into habits, he showed the flexibility of his talent by writing one of the

Beverly Farms, Mass
July 15 1889

Dear Sir, I think it was in
some newspaper that my
first published lines appeared,
and the first "periodical" in
which I wrote was "The
Collegian," a little magazine
published for some six
months in Cambridge in the
year 1830.
                    Yours very truly
                    O W Holmes

wisest and wittiest prose books in the English language. The *Atlantic Monthly* was established in the fall of 1857, and Lowell made it a condition of his acting as editor that Dr. Holmes should be a contributor. Therefore it was that the first number of the new magazine contained the opening pages of the "Autocrat of the Breakfast Table," which every reader followed with delight month after month, until at last the book was completed and published by itself in the fall of 1858. Since then it is rather as a writer of prose than as a writer of verse that Dr. Holmes has been most highly esteemed.

The "Autocrat of the Breakfast Table" is a most original book; but it is not especially original in form, for it is not very unlike the "Spectator" of Addison and Steele, wherein a group of characters is described, and their sayings and doings are duly recorded. In the American book the group of characters meets at the early morning meal, and one of them — the Autocrat himself — does most of the talking. The other figures are lightly sketched — some of them are merely suggested; and even at the very end there is but the thinnest thread of a story.

The real originality of Dr. Holmes's work lay deeper than the external form; it lay in the unaffected simplicity and sincerity of the Autocrat's talk. He seemed rather to be chatting with himself than conversing with others; and no such talk had yet fallen from any American lips — none so cheerful with humor, so laden with thought, so mellow with knowledge, so ripe with experience. The reader was borne along by the current of it, unresisting, smiling often, laughing sometimes, and absorbing always, even if unconsciously, broad and high thoughts about life.

So ample a store of humor — and of good humor — had Dr. Holmes, so well filled a reservoir of sense and of common sense, that he had an abundance of material for other volumes like the "Autocrat." In 1860 he published the "Professor at the Breakfast Table," and in 1872 the "Poet at the Breakfast Table," thus completing the trilogy. Although these two later volumes have not all the freshness of their predecessor, they are inferior only to it; they have the same wholesome spirit, the same sanity, the same sunny sagacity. And these are also the qualities which characterize his last volume of prose, "Over the Teacups," issued in 1890, when he was eighty-one years old.

In all these books there is the precious flavor of actual conversation, the table talk of a broad, liberal, thoughtful man, full of fancy and abounding in humor — a man who could chat with countless readers without raising his voice, speaking softly and easily as though he were seated in his own chimney corner.

Various essays and lighter prose pieces, contributed from time to time to the magazines, he gathered together in 1863 under the apt title of "Soundings from the *Atlantic*." In more than one of these he discussed subjects of everyday life from the point of view of a shrewd and thoughtful physician, avoiding technicalities, and yet using his technical knowledge to help him explain clearly the problem he had in hand.

In 1883, when he made a final revision of all his writings, the best of the papers in this book, with others written afterward, he brought out together as "Pages from an Old Volume of Life." At this time he selected and corrected also a volume of "Medical Essays." Clever as both these books are, with a cleverness of their own, and of a kind no other author possessed, they added but little to Dr. Holmes's reputation. And perhaps it is not unfair to say that this reputation, raised to its highest by the Breakfast Table series, was but little bettered either by the three novels or by the two biographies he wrote after the success of the "Autocrat" tempted him to other ventures in prose.

The three novels were "Elsie Venner," which was published in 1861 ; the "Guardian Angel," which followed

Holmes's Summer Residence, Beverly Farms, Mass.

in 1867; and "A Mortal Antipathy," which came last in 1885. All three of these attempts at story-telling are interesting because they are the work of Dr. Holmes. No one of them is a masterpiece of fiction. He had not received the gift of story-telling in as full a proportion as many novelists without a tithe of his ability. In his hands the novel is rarely dramatic ; it is rather an elaboration of the essay and the character sketch. The teller of the story is more important than the story itself, and his comments are more interesting than his characters.

The strange subjects he chose were suggested to him by his study of his profession ; and the themes of both "Elsie Venner" and "A Mortal Antipathy" are abnormal. Yet in writing fiction, as in writing verses, Dr. Holmes's extraordinary facility stood him in good stead. His stories, whatever their deficiencies in other respects, have all the shrewdness and the insight which always characterize his handling of human character.

The earlier of the two biographies was the memoir of Motley, published in 1878, within two years after the historian's death. Dr. Holmes was one of Motley's oldest comrades, and he told the story of his friend's life and labors with his accustomed skill, although perhaps his tone was a little too apologetic. In the second biography, the memoir of Emerson, published in 1884, he saw no reason to be on the defensive ; and this life is therefore more satisfactory than its predecessor.

Dr. Holmes had, of course, a complete understanding of Emerson's wit, and a full appreciation of Emerson's intelligence, although he had perhaps not so firm a grasp of Emerson's philosophy. Yet the book is delightful. The sage of Concord is presented with the sharpest clearness ; he is made real to us by abundant anecdote ; his works are analyzed with the utmost acumen ; and his career and his character are summed up with absolute sympathy. Both of these biographies were scientifically planned and proportioned, for Dr. Holmes was always the neatest of workmen.

In nothing was he neater than in his characterization of his contemporaries, not only in these two memoirs, but more particularly in the occasional poems which his suc-

cess as a prose writer did not prevent him from producing.
Of Emerson he asked : —

> Where in the realm of thought, whose air is song,
> Does he, the Buddha of the West, belong?
> He seems a wingèd Franklin, sweetly wise,
> Born to unlock the secrets of the skies.

Even happier is his summary of Whittier's character : —

> So fervid, so simple, so loving, so pure,
> We hear but one strain, and our verdict is sure!
> Thee cannot elude us — no further we search —
> 'Tis holy George Herbert cut loose from his church.

And when Lowell went abroad as minister of the United
States to Spain, Holmes rimed this pertinent inquiry : —

> Do you know whom we send you, Hidalgos of Spain?
> Do you know your old friends when you see them again?
> Hosea was Sancho!   You Dons of Madrid,
> But Sancho that wielded the lance of the Cid!

It was the men of Massachusetts that Holmes celebrated in song most freely and most frequently, and although he wrote stirring stanzas of appeal to the whole
United States, west and east, when the life of the nation was
in danger, it was in the little city of Boston that his spirit
resided oftenest.   He it was who declared that "Boston
State House is the hub of the solar system," and that
"you couldn't pry that out of a Boston man if you had the
tire of all creation straightened out for a crowbar."   He
himself was a Bostonian of the strictest sect ; he might
make fun of the little city, but he loved it all the better
for every joke he cracked upon it.

As we turn the pages of the three volumes into which he
finally collected all his verse, it is impossible not to be
struck by the very large proportion of it which is local

in its themes, even if it is not local in its interest. He responded loyally to every call Boston might make upon him, and Boston repaid him with homage and with high praise. It was in Boston that a great public breakfast was given to him in honor of his seventieth birthday. That was in 1879; and three years later he resigned his professorship.

In 1886 he went over to Europe for the second time, almost exactly fifty years after his first visit. He spent the summer in England and France, and he seems to

> And if I should live to be
> The last leaf upon the tree
> In the Spring,
> Let them smile as I do now
> At the old forsaken bough
> Where I cling.
>
> Oliver Wendell Holmes.

have had a very good time indeed, for he kept in age the youthful faculty of enjoyment. From the members of his own profession in England, from the men of letters in London, from the fashionable society of Great Britain, Dr. Holmes received the heartiest welcome; and he was the lion of the London season. He took notes of his travels, recording his observations of men and of manners; and on his return home these jottings were written out, and published the next year as "Our Hundred Days in Europe." It is an easy and a pleasing narrative, rich in the flavor of the author's own personality.

After he had settled down again in Boston, Dr. Holmes continued to write both in prose and in verse. He kept his faculties fully until he had long passed the age of four-score. His final volume of poems, published in 1888, was appropriately called "Before the Curfew," just as Long-fellow and Whittier (also looking to the end) had named their last volumes "In the Harbor" and "At Sundown." Yet after the poems in this collection Holmes wrote those scattered through the pages of "Over the Teacups," which was published in 1890. Four years later he died, on October 7, 1894 — more than sixty years since he had first made himself widely known to his countrymen by the ringing appeal for "Old Ironsides."

Although Holmes had written poems of a wide popu-larity — "Dorothy Q.," "Grandmother's Story of Bunker Hill Battle," the "Wonderful One-Hoss Shay," and the "Broomstick Train" — probably his prose will endure longer than his verse. For his chief quality was intelli-gence, and poetry demands rather imagination. His versa-tility, too, was perhaps more apparent than real, because it was but the result of the dominant intelligence directed into different channels. The force of this intelligence was indisputable ; and Holmes could make it masquerade as wisdom and as knowledge, as shrewdness and as wit — and even as poetry. It is seen at its best in the "Autocrat of the Breakfast Table," and that is why that book is better in kind and in degree than any of its fellows.

With this intelligence Holmes had also absolute sanity —and yet he was not intolerant even toward the bores and the cranks. He had abundant humor, and that helped to sweeten his life and to broaden his influence. Perhaps a certain softening of the asperity of religious debate is due to his preaching and to his practice. To the whole United States he set an example of kindliness and of gentleness, associated with sagacity and with strength. He himself was an exemplar of the amenities he proclaimed. He was the last to survive of the great New England group of authors, Emerson, Longfellow, Hawthorne, Whittier, Holmes, and Lowell, which followed, and in some ways surpassed, the earlier New York group, Irving, Cooper, and Bryant.

QUESTIONS. — In what ways did Holmes give indication, even before he completed his education, of a decided literary bent?

What events showed the attainment by Holmes of maturity in the two kinds of writing in which he was destined to become famous?

In what department of letters did Holmes first make a reputation?

Describe the series of works by which that reputation was at once shifted in field and enlarged in extent.

Compare Holmes's achievements as a novelist with his work as a biographer.

Compare geographically the sympathies of Holmes with those of Whittier and Longfellow.

What events may be mentioned as showing how he was appreciated both at home and abroad?

Is Holmes's fame most likely to be founded hereafter on his prose or on his poetry? Why?

NOTE. — The only complete edition of Holmes's works is that published by Houghton, Mifflin & Co. (13 vols., $19.50). The Cambridge edition contains all the poems in a single volume ($2). "Grandmother's Story of Bunker Hill Battle," etc., and "My Hunt after the Captain," etc., can be had as separate numbers of the Riverside Literature series (15 cents).

The authorized biography is that by Mr. John T. Morse, Jr., now in preparation.

For criticism, see Lowell's "Fable for Critics"; Mr. E. C. Stedman (in his "American Poets"); and Prof. C. F. Richardson (in his history of "American Literature").

## XIV   HENRY DAVID THOREAU

THE little town of Concord has many titles to remembrance. There "the embattled farmers stood and fired the shot heard round the world;" there Emerson wrote "Nature"; there Hawthorne wrote the "Mosses from an Old Manse"; and there was born and lived and died Henry D. Thoreau, an author of even a more marked individuality than either Emerson or Hawthorne. This man was in many ways a true American ; he was free from allegiance to Europe; he was possessed by the democratic spirit. On the other hand, he was content with a mere living ; he had no wish to make money ; he had no desire to get on in the world ; he preferred to limit his own wants and not to be a servant to his own money.

Henry D. Thoreau was born on July 12, 1817. He went to school in Concord and in Boston ; and he entered Harvard College when he was sixteen, graduating in 1837. His family were not well off, and Henry was aided through

Thoreau's Residence, Concord, Mass.

college much as his townsman Emerson had been a few years earlier. He also helped to pay his own way by teaching school. He seems to have been a conscientious student at college ; and he profited by the instruction he received. He was attracted especially by Greek literature, translating some of the tragedies and mastering the lyric poems. Through life he retained a liking for Greek modes of thought and of expression.  As a writer he strove to attain to a Greek clearness and conciseness ; and he succeeded often in achieving a Greek felicity of phrase.  He began early to think for himself, and to keep a journal in which he set down his thoughts and his observations of nature.

Thoreau's family made pencils for a living, and this trade

Henry mastered easily. He was always swift to pick up a handicraft.  He worked also as a carpenter, and occasionally he got a job of surveying. He began to lecture within a year after his graduation from college ; and lecturing was a resource he availed himself of now and again throughout his life.  He wrote poems and prose papers printed by Emer-

Hut on Walden Pond

son in the *Dial*, the short-lived organ of the Transcendentalists.

It was on a piece of land belonging to Emerson, a bit of woodland on the margin of Walden Pond, that Thoreau built himself a shanty in 1845.  In this little hut, a mile from any neighbor, he dwelt for two years and two months. He took up with this way of living because he wished to "transact some private business," so he said.  What he wanted was solitude in which to write out a book, recording his excursion of a week down the Concord and the Merrimac rivers.

He made this account ready for the press during his sojourn in the Walden woods ; and he enlarged his acquaintance with the outdoor world ; and he wrote regularly in his journal. Then when his business was transacted he went back to civilization — never having been out of touch with it for more than a few days at a time. "I left the woods for as good a reason as I went there," he declared. In other words, he had done what he went there to do and he had learnt all that the life alone by Walden Pond could teach him.

At last he succeeded in finding a publisher willing to issue the book he had made ready in his self-enforced solitude in his shanty ; and in 1849 appeared " A Week on the Concord and Merrimac Rivers." It was the account of a journey in which the narrator talked of himself and of his feelings and of his thoughts quite as much as he spoke of the places he passed and of the people he met. Perhaps because of the strangeness of his frank egotism, the book did not then please the public ; and when Thoreau settled finally with the publisher, four years after it had appeared, he took back at least two thirds of the first edition. Without complaint he himself carried the unsold copies upstairs to the garret and then made the characteristically witty entry in his journal, "I have now a library of nearly nine hundred volumes, over seven hundred of which I wrote myself."

Five years after the publication of the "Week," Thoreau issued his second book, the only other volume of his abundant writing to be printed during his own life. He drew from the journal he had kept while he was living in the shanty the material for a book which was published in 1854 as "Walden." This is the work by which Thoreau is best known now and in which his doctrine of life is declared most clearly. The key to Thoreau's philosophy is to be found in his saying that "a man is rich in proportion to the number of things which he can afford to let alone." "I went to the woods," so he tells us, "because I wished to live deliberately, to front only the essential facts of life, and to see if I could not learn what it had to teach, and not, when I came to die, discover that I had not lived."

Some of the readers of "Walden" did not seize the point of this declaration. Whittier wrote to a friend when the book was just published, that he found it "capital reading," but that "the practical moral of it seems to be that if a man is willing to sink himself into a woodchuck he can live as cheaply as that quadruped; but after all, for me, I prefer walking on two legs." Now this is not quite fair, for Thoreau was not sinking himself into a woodchuck when he tried plain living that he might have high thinking; and "Walden" is a most wholesome warning to all those who are willing to let life itself be smothered out of them by the luxuries they have allowed to become necessaries. This is why "Walden" has been called one of the few books of American authorship which it is worth while for an American to read regularly every year.

Thoreau never married; and a man without a wife and without a child can take chances and simplify his life in a way impossible to the man who has given hostages to fortune. Thoreau had little incentive to struggle and to take part in any race for wealth. His wants were always simple and few. If he had but food and warmth and shelter and a book at hand and a friend within an hour's walk he was content. "The cost of a thing," he wrote, "is the amount of what I will call life which is required to be exchanged for it, immediately or in the long run."

In the simplification of his own existence Thoreau was sincere; he followed the bent of his nature. Therefore was Emerson able to write of him after his death, "he was bred to no profession; he never married; he lived alone; he never went to church; he never voted; he refused to pay a tax to the State; he ate no flesh, he drank no wine, he never knew the use of tobacco; and, though a naturalist, he used neither trap nor gun."

His refusal to pay his tax to the State was due to his hatred of slavery and to his unwillingness to be a partner in the government which held slavery to be legal. It was his poll tax that he declined to pay, not his road tax — for that he found the money cheerfully, wishing always to be a good neighbor. After John Brown's vain effort at Harpers Ferry in 1858, Thoreau stood forward in public and told his fellow-citizens of Concord in what high esteem he had held the character of the man whom many have since called the martyr of the anti-slavery cause.

He prepared articles for various magazines, many of which were published during his life and some after his death — which occurred when he was only forty-four. He developed consumption, and long before the end came at last he knew that it would come soon. He suffered especially from sleeplessness, but he faced his fate with fortitude. "His patience was unfailing; assuredly he knew not aught save resignation; he did mightily cheer and console those whose strength was less." He died on May 6, 1862, and he had a public funeral from the Concord church. He was buried in the "Sleepy Hollow," where Hawthorne and Emerson have since joined him.

meet you at R (or before) 12. M.
If the weather is unfavorable,
I will try again — on Friday, &
again. on Monday.

If a storm comes on after starting,
I will seek you at the tavern
in Princeton center, as soon
as circumstances will permit.
I hope you have answered
& closed the bargain.

Yours

Henry D. Thoreau.

Since his death, volume after volume of his writings have been published, some collected from magazines and others extracted from the journal he had kept for thirty years. Two of these books have a certain unity ; one of them is his account of his pioneering adventures in the " Maine Woods," published in 1864; and the other is the somewhat similar record of the several walks he took along the sandy shores of " Cape Cod," published in 1865. Under the apt title of " Excursions " a collection of his scattered papers appeared the year after his death, with a prefatory memoir by his fellow-townsman Emerson, who was fourteen years older than he and who survived him still twenty years.

The observations on nature patiently recorded, day and night, year after year, have been winnowed, and the best of them are now in print in four volumes, " Early Spring in Massachusetts," " Summer," " Autumn," and " Winter." Perhaps it is as a naturalist that Thoreau has the widest reputation. He had an extraordinary familiarity with sylvan life, and the shy creatures of the field and the forest lost some of their shyness with him. He is said to have drawn a woodchuck from its hole by the tail and to have caught a fish in the lake with only his hand. " He knew how to sit immovable, a part of the rock he rested on," so Emerson tells us, "until the bird, the reptile, the fish, which had retired from him, should come back and resume its habits — nay, moved by curiosity, should come to him and watch him." He was a chief of the poet naturalists, and he was not only intimate with nature but friendly. One who knew him said that he talked "about Nature just as if she'd been born and brought up in Concord."

He was always more poet than naturalist, for his observation, interesting as it ever is, is rarely novel. It is his

way of putting what he has seen that takes us rather than
any freshness in the observation itself.  His sentences
have sometimes a Greek perfection ; they have the freshness, the sharpness, and the truth which we find so
often in the writings of the Greeks who came early into
literature, before everything had been seen and said.  Thoreau had a Yankee skill with his fingers, and he could
whittle the English language in like manner ; so he had
also a Greek faculty of packing an old truth into an unexpected sentence.  He was not afraid of exaggeration and
paradox, so long as he could surprise the reader into a
startled reception of his thought.  He was above all an
artist in words, a ruler of the vocabulary, a master phrase-
maker.  But his phrases were all sincere ; he never said
what he did not think ; he was true to himself always.

QUESTIONS. — Speak of the contrasting traits of the third in the trio
of American authors who contributed to make Concord famous.

Show how certain qualities of Thoreau's style as a writer may be
traced to the circumstances of his education.

What is the history of Thoreau's first book?  How did his second
one grow out of this one?

Mention some of the circumstances which seem to justify Thoreau
in his attempts to live up to his theory.

Characterize the work of Thoreau with reference to subject matter
and expression.

NOTE. — The only complete edition of Thoreau's works is that published by
Houghton, Mifflin & Co. (11 vols., $16.50).  The "Succession of Forest Trees,"
etc., with biographical sketch by Emerson, can be had as a separate number of the
Riverside Literature series (Houghton, Mifflin & Co., 15 cents).

There are biographies by Mr. H. A. Page and Mr. F. B. Sanborn, who has also
edited Thoreau's letters.

For criticism, see Emerson's sketch; Lowell (in "My Study Windows") ; Mr.
T. W. Higginson (in "Short Studies of American Authors") ; R. L. Stevenson
(in "Familiar Studies of Men and Books") ; Mr. John Burroughs (in "Indoor
Studies") ; and Prof. Richardson (in his history of "American Literature").

## XV  JAMES RUSSELL LOWELL

THE Lowells have always held an honored place in the
local history of New England.   One member of the family
introduced cotton-spinning into the United States ; and
for him the town of Lowell in Massachusetts is named.
Another left money to found in Boston the course of
lectures known as the Lowell Institute.   The most distinguished of them all was James Russell Lowell, who
was born in 1819 at Cambridge, Massachusetts, on February 22 — the birthday of the most distinguished of all
Americans.

His father was a Boston clergyman of high character and fine training, and his mother, who was descended from an Orkney family, had an ardent appreciation of poetry and romance, which she was able to transmit to her children. The boy grew to manhood in Cambridge, then little more than a straggling village. There he went to a dame school : —

> Propped on the marsh, a dwelling now, I see,
> The humble schoolhouse of my A, B, C,
> Where well-drilled urchins, each behind his tire,
> Waited in ranks the wished command to fire ;
> Then all together, when the signal came,
> Discharged their *a-b abs* against the dame,
> She, 'mid the volleyed learning, firm and calm,
> Patted the furloughed ferule on her palm,
> And, to our wonder, could divine at once
> Who flashed the pan, and who was downright dunce.

At the age of eight or nine he was sent as a day pupil to a boarding school in Cambridge, where the boys were made to work hard. To the training and to the instructions received at this school Lowell owed much in after life. It happened that two or three of the letters he wrote then to a brother away from home have been kept, and they show that he was already fond of books, often thinking about them and always glad to get them. In one letter written before he was ten he tells his brother that their mother has just given him three volumes of Scott's "Tales of a Grandfather," and he declares "I have got quite a library."

At the age of fifteen he entered Harvard. This was in 1834, and in 1836 Longfellow came to the college to teach literature, succeeding Ticknor, the historian of Spanish literature — as Lowell was to succeed Longfellow a score of years later. At Harvard Lowell was not a diligent student; he liked better to read what interested him than to master the tasks set before him by the college authorities. Spenser was already a favorite poet of his, and he seems early to have entered on the study of Dante, which was to be a life-long pleasure to him.

He began to rime himself, and in his junior year he wrote the anniversary poem. He was made editor of the college magazine in his senior year. He seems to have been popular with his classmates and he was chosen to write the class poem. But he had so neglected certain of the prescribed studies of the college that he was suspended for several months, and as the term of suspension extended over class-day, he was not able himself to deliver the poem he had written. He had it printed for his companions, although he held it in too slight esteem ever to include it among the poems of his maturity.

After his graduation he thought of entering the Divinity School, but he decided at last to study law. Although he was on the very verge of giving it up twenty times, he persevered and received his degree of Bachelor of Laws in 1840. He opened an office in Boston, but it is doubtful whether he ever had even that first client whom he was afterward to describe in a humorous sketch. With no great liking for the law as a means of livelihood, he finally abandoned it, as Holmes had done only a few years earlier.

Lowell had become engaged to Miss Maria White, who was to influence the whole course of his life. The first result of his happy love was the publication in 1841 of a volume of poems, some of which had been printed already in the magazines, and others were hasty and crude rimes which he kept out of later editions of his poems — just as

Whittier rejected his own early verses. Lowell was barely twenty-two when this book appeared, but there was more than one poem in it which gave high promise of his future. In addition to his ability, he had a deep love for letters; and this it was which led him a year later to start a monthly magazine. In his ardor and in his inexperience he made this periodical too exclusively literary to attain a wide popularity; and, unfortunately, after three numbers it came to an end suddenly, leaving its projectors in debt.

In his class poem Lowell had shown himself lacking in sympathy with the Transcendentalists and with the Abolitionists; and until he met Miss White his interests and his ambitions were almost wholly literary. Under her influence his higher nature developed and he came to have a strong feeling for the fellow human beings who were held in bondage. He swiftly saw that in real life there were causes to be fought far better worth the struggle than any mere craving for personal fame. His love for letters never lessened, but it was linked thereafter to the love for human freedom.

He was married at last in 1844, in which year he brought out a revised edition of his poems. A few months later he gathered from the magazines certain prose criticisms, chiefly about the older English poets — criticisms which he thought so lightly of in later years that he did not allow them to be included in his collected works. And about this time he was a frequent contributor to the *Pennsylvania Freeman*, the antislavery journal formerly edited by Whittier.

Settled at Cambridge in Elmwood (the beautiful old house where he had been born), happily married, supporting himself by his writings and enlisted in the service of a cause which he had taken to heart, Lowell was able to conquer his native indolence. He undertook to contribute every week, either in prose or in verse, to one of the ablest of the antislavery journals; and he kept this agreement for nearly four years, from 1846 to 1850. These were four years of unrest and excitement throughout the world; and here in the United States the discussion over slavery became more and more acute.

Elmwood

Chiefly to gain an increase of territory for the expansion of slavery, this country was involved in a war with Mexico over the admission of Texas. Although it is easy enough now to see that we needed the new lands we were to gain by force of arms, and that without them the proper expansion of the United States was not possible, it was hard to foresee this then. What was obvious at that time was that both the motives and the methods of those who were urging us into the Mexican war were alike unworthy. This is what Lowell saw with his usual keenness; and no one attacked those responsible for the Mexican war more sharply than he or more effectively.

The weapon he chose was satiric verse written in the homely dialect of the New England farmer. With pungent humor and in stanzas that had a sharp flavor of the soil, "Hosea Biglow" made fun of the attempts to rouse his fellow-citizens to military fervor. His stinging lines, which scorched themselves into the memory, were accompanied by the prose comments of "Parson Wilbur," who represented the other side of the New England character. While the clergyman was glad to air his culture and his classics, he served admirably to set off the simple frankness of the Yankee youth.

That the lyrics of Hosea should linger in the ears of those who heard them, Lowell took care to give to each a swinging rhythm and often also a catching refrain. When at last the scattered "Biglow Papers" were collected into a volume in 1848, the author, just to show that the New England dialect was serviceable for other things than satire, added to the book a Yankee idyl, "The Courtin'," one of the most beautifully natural love episodes in all English poetry.

During these same years of political turmoil while he was writing the "Biglow Papers" one after another, Lowell produced another satire of a very different kind, the "Fable for Critics," which was also published in 1848; it was purely literary in its outlook; it was a consideration in verse of the state of American literature at the end of the first half of the nineteenth century. It contained a gallery of portraits of the American authors then prominent; and in every portrait the characteristic features of the original were seized with swift insight and reproduced with sharp vigor.

It is a proof of Lowell's excellence of judgment and of his independence of attitude, that the opinions he expressed about the leading American authors of that time coincide closely with that on which the best criticism is now agreed fifty years later.   And the rattling lines of the poem are as readable now as when they were first written, with their scattering fire of verbal jokes, of ingenious rimes, and of personal witticisms.   As the "Biglow Papers" is the firmest and the finest political satire yet written in the United States, so the "Fable for Critics" is the clearest and most truthful literary satire.

Nor did these two satires withdraw him wholly from the higher poetry on which his heart was set.   And in this same year, 1848, he sent forth also the "Vision of Sir Launfal," his first attempt at telling a story in verse.   It is the best of all his serious poems ; perhaps loftier in conception and more careful in execution.  His habit then, as always, was to brood over the subject he wished to treat in verse, to fill himself with it, to work himself up to a white heat over it, and finally to write it out at a single sitting if possible.   He rarely revised and his verse lacked finish and polish, though it never wanted force.   It was at this time that he told Longfellow he meant to give up poetry because he could "not write slowly enough."

His poetry also suffered from another failing of his.   He was not content to set forth beauty only and to let the reader discover a moral for himself.   Like Longfellow sometimes and like Whittier often, Lowell insisted unduly on the burden of his song.   And he knew his own defect and wrote later in life, "I shall never be a poet till I get out of the pulpit, and New England was all meetinghouse when I was growing up." In the "Fable for Critics"(which was published without his own name as author, and in which he thought it best to include himself among the poets satirized) he thus judges his own efforts : —

> There is Lowell, who's striving Parnassus to climb —
> With a whole bale of isms tied together with rime ;
> He might get on alone, spite of brambles and boulders,
> But he can't with that bundle he has on his shoulders ;
> The top of the hill he will ne'er come nigh reaching
> Till he learns the distinction 'twixt singing and preaching ;
> His lyre has some chords that would ring pretty well,
> But he'd rather by half make a drum of the shell,
> And rattle away till he's old as Methusalem,
> At the head of a march to the last new Jerusalem.

During these years when Lowell was making his way as a poet and when he was happy in his work, the health of his wife was slowly fading. For her sake they went to Europe in 1851, returning the following year. In spite of all that could be done for her she died in October, 1853. As it happened, a daughter was born to Longfellow on the day of the death of Lowell's wife, and in the lovely poem of the "Two Angels" the elder poet tried to console the younger.

> Angels of Life and Death alike are His ;
> Without His leave they pass no threshold o'er :
> Who, then, would wish or dare, believing this,          ¬
> Against His messengers to shut the door?

In the fall of 1854 Lowell delivered a series of lectures on the English poets. These addresses, given at the Lowell Institute in Boston, revealed all the richness and strength of his culture and displayed the full power of his critical faculty. They proved that he was the American critic who had at once the keenest insight and the widest equipment. Almost immediately after he had made these discourses and entirely without his own solicitation he was offered the professorship of modern languages at Harvard, which Longfellow had just resigned. He accepted this arduous and honorable position in the oldest American university, and he was allowed two years' leave of absence to spend in Europe in study. So it was in the spring of 1857 that Lowell became a professor of Harvard — just ten years after Dr. Holmes had begun his own connection with that institution.

With Dr. Holmes he was soon brought into closer contact. A new American magazine was planned, to contain contributions more particularly from the New England group of writers ; and the editorship was offered to Lowell. The first number of the *Atlantic* which appeared in 1857 contained the opening paper of the "Autocrat of the Breakfast Table" ; and for four years Lowell edited this magazine, toiling faithfully, writing abundantly himself, generally on political themes, and encouraging new writers of ability. After he resigned the editorship of the *Atlantic* he became for a while one of the conductors of the *North American Review*, the venerable quarterly to which Bryant had contributed "Thanatopsis" nearly half a century before. Under the title of "Fireside Travels" he published in 1864 a volume of his prose papers collected chiefly from the magazines.

But long before this peaceful prose appeared, Lowell had been moved again to express in verse his feelings and his thoughts on the times. "Hosea Biglow" had come into being during the Mexican war ; and it was the Civil War which evoked him once more. Love of country was the core of Lowell's character and the outbreak of the Rebellion stirred his nature to its depths.

The second series of the "Biglow Papers," written at intervals during the war, met with even wider popular approval than the first series ; and certainly the stinging stanzas of "Jonathan to John" are unsurpassed in all English satire. When this second series of the "Biglow Papers" were collected into a volume in 1867 Lowell prefixed to it a consideration of the past, the present, and the future of the English language in America — a paper which had scholarship equal to its humor and a sweetness of temper equal to both — a paper to be read by all who want to understand how it is that we Americans own a whole and undivided half of the English language.

In 1869 Lowell made a collection of his graver verse, "Under the Willows," in which he included his more serious poems of the war. Among them were the thrilling lines of the "Washers of the Shroud," and the noble and lofty ode recited at the Harvard Commemoration of those of her students who had fallen in battle for the right — the ode in which the poet set forth in imperishable phrase the true character of Abraham Lincoln. And in this same year Lowell also put forth the longest of his single poems, the "Cathedral," a work in which the parts are greater than the whole, and which is rather Gothic than Greek in conception and execution. It is elevated in its purpose, and yet there is an occasional obtrusion of prankish humor not unlike the grotesque faces which grin down on the visitor to the actual cathedral at Chartres.

From the many critical papers which he had written, chiefly for the periodicals he had edited, and which were often founded on courses of college lectures, Lowell made a first choice in 1870, and published "Among my Books," a volume of prose essays in criticism. The year after, another volume appeared called "My Study Windows";

and a few years later came yet another, the second series of "Among my Books." In the final edition of his writings the contents of these three volumes has been rearranged somewhat. Among them were the criticisms of the great poets Dante, Spenser, Shakspere, Milton, Wordsworth; cordial papers on Lowell's own favorites, Dryden, Lessing, and Keats; and pungent yet mellow essays "On a Certain Condescension in Foreigners," on "My Garden Acquaintance," and on "A Good Word for Winter."

As these volumes proved, Lowell was the greatest of all American critics of literature. He had knowledge and wisdom, culture and sagacity. His writing has the leisurely amplitude of the scholar and the sharp thrust of the wit. The gift of the winged phrase was his; and no man of our time ever packed truth oftener into an epigram. He had also the wide and deep acquaintance with literature which is the best backbone of criticism. So fine was his scholarship, and so broad his cultivation, that he was wholly devoid of petty pedantries; he had too sure a sense of proportion to confuse trifling facts with truths of real importance.

Lowell had enjoyed heartily his own frequent reading of the works of the great authors he wrote about, and he was able to convey some of this enjoyment to his own readers, and to explain to them the reasons for his liking. His favorite of all was the mighty Florentine poet Dante, whom he steadily studied from early life. Indeed, the advice he gave to young men seeking culture was to find the great writer whom they most appreciated and to give themselves to the constant perusal of this great writer, growing up to him slowly and discovering gradually that to understand him adequately would force them sooner or later to learn many of the things best worth learning.

When the time came to celebrate the centenary of the chief events of the Revolution, Lowell was the poet to whom the American people turned to have their thoughts and their sentiments voiced for them in verse ; and Lowell delivered an ode at the centenary of the fight at Concord Bridge, and another at the centenary of Washington's taking command of the American army at Cambridge just before the siege of Boston, and a third on the Fourth of July, 1876. In this same year these " Three Memorial Poems " were published together in a single volume.

The next year he was called to the service of the country whose foundation he had been celebrating in song. He was sent in 1877 as American Minister to Spain, where another man of letters, Washington Irving, had preceded him half a century before. In 1880 he was transferred from Madrid to London.

No American minister ever made himself more welcome among a foreign people than Lowell made himself among the British. And his popularity was not due to any attempt to please their prejudices ; Lowell abated not a jot or tittle of his Americanism — rather on occasion did he accentuate it. In sending him to Great Britain the United States sent the best we had. Our kin across the sea were quick to understand the opportunity offered to them ; and by their request Lowell delivered in England many public addresses, some of them formal orations, while others were but offhand after dinner speeches. But whatever the occasion, Lowell was equal to it, never more amply than when he went to Birmingham to make an exposition of the theory and practice of " Democracy " in America. Nowhere more plainly than in England was Lowell's Americanism seen to be ingrained. With him patriotism was almost a passion.

He remained in England three years and then returned home, and Dr. Holmes greeted him with a copy of verses, in which he asked, —

> By what enchantments, what alluring arts,
> Our truthful James led captive British hearts, —
> Whether his shrewdness made their statesmen halt,
> Or if his learning found their dons at fault,
> Or if his virtue was a strange surprise,
> Or if his wit flung sawdust in their eyes, —
> Like honest Yankees we can simply guess;
> But that he did it, all must needs confess.
> England herself without a blush may claim
> Her only conqueror since the Norman came.

After his return to his native land Lowell revised the most important of the many addresses he had delivered in England, and in 1886 he published them in a single volume under the title of the full and rich discourse in which he had declared the better side of "Democracy." Here at home Lowell never hesitated to point out the shortcomings of his countrymen, their errors and their blunders; but when he was abroad it was on their merits only that he was willing to dwell. In the address on "Democracy" he had told the British all that was best in our social system; and when he came home he made haste to tell us Americans how we must labor to remove all that is evil in our social system. He did this in a speech on the "Independent in Politics," and this address was included in a volume of "Political Essays" published in 1888.

In this same year appeared also his last volume of poetry, "Heartsease and Rue." In verse as in prose, Lowell was nearly always an improviser, pouring forth suddenly in a single powerful jet all that he had been slowly bringing to a white heat within him. He lacked the patient

God of our fathers, Thou who wast
Art, & shalt be when the Eyes-wise who float
Thy secret presence shall be lost
In the great light that dazzles them to doubt,
We, sprung from loins of stalwart men
Whose strength was in their trust
That Thou wouldst make thy dwelling in their dust
And walk with them a fellow-citizen
Who build a city of the just,
We, who believe Life's bases rest
Beyond the probe of chemic test,
Still, like our fathers, feel thee near
Sure that, while lasts the immutable decree,
The land to Human Nature dear
Shall not be unbeloved of Thee.

toil of the artist who should not only file and polish, but if need be recast altogether. He worked too hastily for perfection of finish. The "Biglow Papers" have a tunefulness and a rhythmic swing lacking to most of his more serious poems. Some of these later verses have lightness and ease ; and they have also their share of the humorous shrewdness and the witty pith for which the "Biglow Papers" are unsurpassed in all English literature.

As Lowell drew near to the allotted limit of threescore years and ten he was everywhere recognized as one of the foremost citizens of the republic, a type of the character most needed in American public life — the man of broad culture, having a solid understanding of his fellow-men and a deep love of his country. Probably the later years of his life were made pleasanter by this atmosphere of appreciation. At last his health failed and he died on August 12, 1891, being then seventy-two years old.

Of the New England group of American authors, Lowell, although survived by both Whittier and Holmes, was the youngest except Parkman. All of these except Hawthorne and Parkman were poets, and the fame of Longfellow and Whittier may be said to be due wholly to their poetry. Lowell, like Emerson, was a poet also, but his work in prose was at least equal in value to his work in verse. He was the one great literary critic of the group, as Hawthorne was the one great story-teller.

QUESTIONS. — What are the points of interest in Lowell's life to the time of his marriage?

What was his wife's influence in shaping his future career?

Upon what occasion and with what weapons did Lowell make his first appearance in the political arena?

In what striking literary work did he show the soundness of his literary judgment?

From what two failings did Lowell's poetry suffer?

In what work did Lowell present an interesting mixture of linguistic knowledge and poetical satire?

What is the character of the volume in which he included a poem the parts of which are said to be greater than the whole?

Discuss the qualities displayed by Lowell in the collections of essays published in the '70's.

To what positions was Lowell appointed? And how did he serve in these posts?

Tell about Lowell's career after his return to America.

NOTE. — The complete edition of Lowell's works is that published by Houghton, Mifflin & Co. (12 vols., $17.50). The Cambridge edition contains all the poems in a single volume ($2). "Under the Old Elm," etc., the "Vision of Sir Launfal," etc., and "Books and Libraries," etc., can be had as separate numbers of the Riverside Literature series (Houghton, Mifflin & Co., 15 cents).

There is a biography by F. H. Underwood. The "Letters," edited by Prof. C. E. Norton (Harper & Bros., 2 vols., $8) is almost an autobiography.

For criticism, see Mr. E. C. Stedman (in "American Poets"); Prof. C. F. Richardson (in his history of "American Literature"); Prof. Barrett Wendell (in "Stelligeri"); Mr. Henry James (in "Essays in London"); and Prof. George E. Woodberry (in the *Century*, November, 1891).

## XVI   FRANCIS PARKMAN

It is not often that a man who forms a high purpose in his youth loyally devotes his whole life to its accomplishment, and finally survives just long enough to see that it is achieved. This, however, is what Francis Parkman did. When he was still but a boy in college he resolved to tell the story of the long struggle between the French and the English for the possession of North America. To this task he gave himself his whole life long; and when the work was done at last, after the unhasting labor of nearly half a century, he was ready to die, being then about seventy years of age. And this singular success was won in the face of difficulties which would have discouraged any man who had not very unusual firmness of fiber.

Francis Parkman was born in Boston on September 16, 1823. He belonged to what Dr. Holmes called the " Brahmin caste of New England," that is to say, his ancestors had been men of education and character generation after generation. The family had endowed two professorships at Harvard College.

In his boyhood Parkman's health was not robust ; and he was sent to live in the country on the edge of the wild tract known as Middlesex Fells. Here he spent four years in intimate acquaintance with the forest. Then after proper schooling he entered Harvard College ; and it was when he was a sophomore that he formed the purpose of writing the history of the French and Indian War — a design which easily expanded later into that of telling the story of the whole conflict between the French and the English in North America. And from the day when this project first took shape in the mind of the young man at college, everything he did afterwards was made to contribute to its fulfillment.

In one college vacation he camped and canoed in the backwoods of Maine, and in another he was able to explore all the recesses of Lake George and Lake Champlain. Even an accident in the gymnasium happened to help on his preparation for his work; because he made a voyage of recovery to Europe, and in Rome he lodged for a while in a monastery, thus getting to know more about the character and the training of the self-sacrificing priests whose devotion to duty he had afterward to chronicle. On his return home he rejoined his class and was graduated in 1844. For two years he seems to have studied law with more or less persistence. As it happened, his grand-father had made a fortune; and there was therefore no immediate pressure on Parkman to set about earning his own living.

Then he took a long journey to help fit himself for the task before him. He needed to know the Indians and to understand their enigmatic character. He wanted also to study the frontiersmen, whose ways differ but little from those of their forefathers three or four generations ago, since like conditions are sure to produce men of like characteristics. In the time of the French and Indian War the red savage and the white borderer had been both of them close to the Atlantic coast; but toward the middle of the nineteenth century the advance of civilization had pressed them back over the Alleghanies and across the Mississippi. It was to the Rocky Mountains that Park-man went in 1846 with a friend, spending a summer with the Sioux in their camps among the Black Hills of Dakota and on the vast tableland through which the Platte River twists itself languidly.

He and his friend lived with the Indians, sharing their rough fare and studying their ways and their customs, and getting an insight into their character not to be had in any other manner. They underwent also the hardships of the Indians, the toils, the privations, the exposure; and Park-man was so enfeebled by these that he never regained his strength. While with the Indians he was so ill that he had to be lifted into his saddle, and it was only because his will was firm enough to give him the mastery even over pain that he was able to get back to civilization. And when at last he made his way home he was perma-nently disabled; and for three years he was unable to use his eyes.

To the friend who had been with him in these Western wanderings he dictated a record of their experiences. This, after being printed in a magazine, was published in 1849 in a volume known now as the "Oregon Trail." It is one of the very best books of outdoor adventure ever written and one of the most valuable, for it has preserved for us the outward appearance of a state of things long since vanished forever. From it the reader can gain an understanding of the red men and of their white neighbors, and a knowledge of the motives which rule their conduct, unobtainable from any other single book. It helps us to explain to ourselves the unending series of wars between the white race and the red, ever since the men of our stock first set foot on the soil which the Indian claimed for his own. It enables us to see for ourselves that the Indian Cooper presented in his novels is very like the real Indian, but that the real Indian had another side to him than the side Cooper chose to depict.

His inherited means relieved Parkman from the necessity of writing for money, and it allowed him to undertake a long task not likely to pay him a full pecuniary reward even at the end. To many a young man with broken health this money might have been merely a temptation to luxurious idleness ; to many another it would have afforded an excuse for toying with literature as an amateur only ; to Parkman it yielded the opportunity for strenuous labor. Without his inherited wealth it would have been impossible for Parkman to have accomplished anything, since he was dependent on others for the things which other authors are able to do for themselves.

For forty years and more he led what he himself called a life of "repressed activity." His eyes had failed him ; and he was aware that his mind might fail him also if he worked it hard. There were years when he was not allowed to work at all. There were years when he was able to read only for one minute at a time, resting the next minute and reading again the third and so on for half an hour, and when three or four of these broken half hours were all the reading he was allowed during the day. Of course he could not write ; and all his histories were dictated to a member of his family, who prepared them for the press.

The first book he composed after the publication of the  " Oregon Trail " was an account of the cleverly planned Indian rising which in 1763 came so near to undoing the English victories over the French. This " History of the Conspiracy of Pontiac," published in 1851, is really a supplement to the main history of the struggle of the French and English for North America. Perhaps Parkman wrote it first

Parkman's Residence, Boston, Mass.

because he was then fresh from actual contact with the Indians, and perhaps because he wished to try his 'prentice hand at a less important book before beginning his great work.

It is almost inconceivable that he was able to accomplish anything under the difficulties which held him fast ;

but he devised in time a method of work which enabled him to overcome them finally. He made it a point always to see for himself the scene of every event he had to describe; and his descriptions of scenery are always lucid and graphic, sympathetic and picturesque. He collected all the books bearing in any way on the matter he had in hand, all histories, biographies, journals, accounts of all kinds. He had copies made for him of all the unprinted documents, private letters, official reports, and public statements, wherever these might be, in the libraries of America or in the government collections of France and Great Britain or in the personal archives of old families. He had the aid of competent assistants who read all the documents aloud to him twice, once that he might form in his own mind an outline of the story, and a second time that he might secure the salient details. As these documents were read he took notes or he had them taken.

Thus slowly, laboriously, he was able to piece together the story he wanted to tell. Probably the apparent disadvantage of the method he had to adopt was a real advantage, for it forced him to digest his materials absolutely, to think out to the end before he started on the beginning, to carry in his head the entire story complete in all its parts and proportioned properly. But though the result repaid him, the limitations under which he labored were very severe.

A friend has described him as always "waiting for moments of health as his greatest blessing, glad to do a little, and always thankful when he could do more. He could not go into society, because it consumed his strength. He could see but few friends in his own house, for the same reason. His own family had to shield him

from excitements.  It was like fighting destiny to do anything, and yet month by month the noiseless fabric grew,
and book after book was published, until his plan was
completed."

The general title which he gave finally to his great work
was "France and England in North America."  The successive seven books were each complete in themselves and
yet all fitted together to make a compact whole.  They
were not published in a strictly chronological order, because as Parkman grew in years he wished at least to
leave behind him the most important divisions of the
work; but he lived to pick up all the parts passed
over.

The first to appear was the volume on the " Pioneers of
France in the New World," which is the opening of the
series and which was published in 1865.  In 1867 came
the second book, on the "Jesuits in North America in the
Seventeenth Century," a narrative of heroic and fruitless
endeavor, followed two years later by "La Salle; or the
Discovery of the Great West."  Then there was an inter-
val of five years before the book on the "Old Régime in
Canada" appeared in 1874.  Three years later came
"Count Frontenac and New France under Louis XIV."
The two books which conclude the series, and which were
published in reverse order, are "A Half Century of Conflict," issued in 1892, and " Montcalm and Wolfe," issued
in 1884.

No finer subject could any historian have than this conflict of France and England for the possession of North
America; and no finer history has been written by any man
of our time.  It has the twofold merit that it can be read
with pleasure and it can be relied on with confidence.
Parkman first made himself master of all the facts and then

Dear Sir,

To the best of my recollection the Journal of Nathaniel Woodhull was printed either in the publications of the Essex Institute or in the old Historical Magazine. It is not of great value, and I have searched in vain for the reference to it among my notes, which are at present in some disorder.

Yours sincerely
F. Parkman

Boston,
2 Dec '84

217

he selected those which were essential and set them forth in most interesting fashion.

In his reliance on research he was rigidly scientific; in his presentation of the results of his research he was unfailingly artistic. He sought truth always, and having found it he tried to present it as beauty also. For every fact, every allusion, every picturesque touch, he could give his authority; but he did not heap up his investigations crudely and make his readers form impressions of their own. He showed to the world the carved statue perfect in its strength and in its grace; he did not draw attention to the models he used, to the rough block he had hewn, or to the scattered chips of the workshop.

Parkman was happily married in 1852; but he lost his wife in 1858, after which he lived with his sister in Boston, either in the center of the city or in its outskirts on the shore of Jamaica Pond. In this latter place he was able to be outdoors and to become expert as a plant-grower, even originating new species. He wrote a book about roses; and for a year or two he was professor of horticulture at Harvard. He used to say that his garden had saved his life.

After the completion of his history in 1892 he began at once the revision of the earliest volumes in the light of his later labors. In this pleasant task he was engaged when he died on September 8, 1893. His work was done and he could die happy.

After his death Holmes summed up his labors in a poem of which these stanzas may be quoted here : —

> He told the red man's story; far and wide
>   He searched the unwritten records of his race;
> He sat a listener at the Sachem's side,
>   He tracked the hunter through his wildwood chase.

High o'er his head the soaring eagle screamed;
  The wolf's long howl rang nightly; through the vale
Tramped the lone bear; the panther's eyeballs gleamed;
  The bison's gallop thundered on the gale.

Soon o'er the horizon rose the cloud of strife —
  Two proud, strong nations battling for the prize —
Which swarming host should mold a nation's life,
  Which royal banner flout the western skies.

Long raged the conflict; on the crimson sod
  Native and alien joined their hosts in vain;
The lilies withered where the Lion trod,
  Till Peace lay panting on the ravaged plain.

QUESTIONS. — What is there remarkable about the life and works of Parkman?

How was the usual history of a well-born Boston boy varied in his case?

Describe the events of the long journey which Parkman took in order to help fit himself for the task which he had already set before him.

Compare the subject of Parkman's first book, as it was presented by him, with the same theme as it was pictured by an earlier American novelist.

Describe the methods by which alone Parkman was enabled to complete his great undertaking.

Describe the work that gives to Parkman a valid claim to be ranked with the foremost historians in the nineteenth century.

How was his work summed up by Holmes?

NOTE. — The complete edition of Parkman's works is that published by Little, Brown & Co. (12 vols., $18). They issued also a cheap edition of the "Oregon Trail" ($1).

Mr. Charles H. Farnham has written Parkman's biography (Little, Brown & Co., $2.50), and Prof. John Fiske is preparing a Life for the American Men of Letters series. For a fragment of autobiography see the *Harvard Graduates' Magazine* for May, 1895.

For criticism, see Lowell and Mr. Edward Eggleston (in the *Century* for November, 1892).

# XVII  OTHER WRITERS

THE authors who have been considered, one by one, in the preceding chapters are not the only American men of letters whose writings are still read; but they are the writers with whose works the youth of the United States ought soonest to become acquainted. There were always other literators laboring side by side with these more distinguished authors, overshadowed by them and yet deserving of remembrance. There were also men of prominence in other callings than literature, who took up the pen now and again to advance a cause in which they were interested.

Not a few of the early state papers of our country have literary merit in a high degree. The Declaration of Independence, for example, written by Thomas Jefferson (1743–1826), afterwards President of the United States, combines most skillfully brilliant rhetoric and compact logic; and the Constitution of the United States, the result of the united wisdom of the foremost statesmen of the day, owes much of its clearness and its force to Gouverneur Morris (1752–1816), who made the final revision of its vigorous English.

In arousing the public spirit which enabled us to achieve our independence no single effort was perhaps more effective than an appeal called "Common Sense," written by Thomas Paine (1737–1809) and published in 1776; and the author followed it up with the successive issues of a periodical, the *Crisis*, which were also useful to the patriotic cause.

After the revolution was accomplished and after the necessity was felt for a strong and yet flexible form of government, the proposed constitution might not have been adopted if it had not been ex-plained and defended by a series of papers published from time to time in 1787–88 under the general title of the *Federalist*. These are, perhaps, the ablest political essays in the Eng-lish language ; and they are like some of the great speeches of Burke, in that they were intended to effect an immediate purpose only and yet have served ever since as a perpetual store-

Alexander Hamilton

house of political wisdom.  They were written by Alex-ander Hamilton (1757–1804), John Jay (1745–1829), and

Daniel Webster

James Madison (1751–1836). After the adoption of the con-stitution Hamilton became Sec-retary of the Treasury under Washington, whom he after-wards aided in preparing the " Farewell Address."   Jay was the first Chief Justice of the Supreme Court ; and Madison was the fourth President of the United States.

Two other American states-men cannot be omitted from any survey of American literature, however brief.  The first of these is Daniel Webster (1782–1852), the most famous of American public speakers, and perhaps the only American who could challenge comparison with the great orators of Europe. One idea runs through all Webster's speeches — the greatness and the glory of this American Union and the necessity of preserving it forever. This is really the theme of his two solemn and stately orations at Bunker Hill, one delivered when the foundation stone of the monument was laid in 1825, and the other when the monument was completed in 1843.

The second of the American statesmen holding high rank as a man of letters was Abraham Lincoln (1809–1865), whose later state papers are models, not only in insight and in tact but in expression also. His masterpiece is the short speech delivered on the battlefield of Gettysburg at the dedication of the national cemetery in November, 1863. Lofty in thought, deep in feeling, simple in language, this speech has a Greek perfection of form.

It is but a short step now to take up the men who have written history in America, after dealing thus briefly with those who helped to make history here. In 1834 Jared

Sparks (1789–1866) wrote a life of Washington and edited the letters and other papers of our first President; and he afterward did a like service for other worthies of the Revolutionary period. He preserved for us much valuable material which might otherwise have been lost, but he liked to show his heroes always in full dress, and he omitted facts and altered texts the better to sustain the dignity of history as he understood it.

George Bancroft

In the same year that Sparks published the first volume of his " Washington," George Bancroft (1800–1891) published the first volume of his massive "History of the United States," a monument of honorable labor and intellectual effort, the tenth and last volume of which was not completed until 1874 — forty years after the book had begun to appear. Bancroft also took part in public affairs, and when Secretary of the Navy he established the Naval Academy now at Annapolis ; when collector of the port of Boston he gave an appointment to Hawthorne. He was also minister to Great Britain in 1846, and twenty years later he was minister to Germany.

Another historian, John Lothrop Motley (1814–1877), was our minister to Austria at one time and afterward to Great Britain. He chose for the subject of his studies the rise of the brave little Dutch republic from which the people of the United States have derived so many of their institutions. The first book he devoted to this thrilling theme was published in 1854. After his death his life was written by his friend, Dr. Holmes.

An even more interesting period of history was selected by William Hickling Prescott (1796–1859), who examined the condition of Spain at the time Columbus set forth to discover a new world. This book on " Ferdinand and Isabella " was published in 1837 and it was followed within ten years by books on the Spanish "Conquest of Mexico" and "Conquest of Peru," two of the most marvelous true stories to be found anywhere in the annals of mankind.

William H. Prescott

A friend of Motley's and the editor of his letters was George William Curtis (1824–1892), who was perhaps after Lowell the most charming of American essayists. Curtis wrote a novel or two and a social satire ; he was for years

a popular lecturer; but his strength is best revealed in the
many addresses he delivered, in which he upheld a lofty
ideal of American citizenship.    Three other essayists may
also be mentioned here, George Ripley (1802–1880), who
took part in the Brook Farm experiment with Hawthorne
and Curtis, and who did much to further scholarship in the
United States; E. P. Whipple (1819–1886), who was a
Boston lecturer and critic; and Richard Grant White
(1821–1885), who edited Shakspere's works and who wrote
frequently about the misuse of words.

Critics and essayists also were the two poets N. P.

Bayard Taylor

Willis and Bayard Taylor.  Willis
(1806–1867) was a journalist, who
when he was barely out of boyhood
wrote a series of blank verse poems
on scriptural themes, which were received at once with high praise.   Bayard Taylor was also a journalist, who
began his literary career by letters of
travel.   He wished always to be a poet,
but perhaps his most valuable poetic
effort was his metrical translation of
Goethe's "Faust."

J. G. Saxe (1816–1887) was a poet who wrote society
verse of not a little sparkle, although not equal to the best
in that kind by Halleck and by Holmes.   Two Southern
poets must not be passed over, Henry Timrod (1829–1867)
and Sidney Lanier (1842–1881), both of whom died before
their allotted time, partly because of the weakness brought
on by exposure while they were fighting for the lost cause.

Greater than any of these was Walt Whitman (1819–
1892), who is even called by some foreign critics the greatest of all American poets.   Whitman was an intense Amer-

ican, renouncing all allegiance to the past and looking to the future with splendid confidence. His stalwart verse was irregular, but often it was beautifully rhythmic. No one of the many tributes to Lincoln, not even Lowell's noble eulogy, is more deeply charged with exalted feeling than Whitman's "O Captain, My Captain."

Walt Whitman

Curtis and Taylor and Willis were all writers of fiction, although no one of them made his reputation by a novel. The earliest American romancer was Charles Brockden Brown (1771–1810), a Philadelphian whose strange and gloomy tales, pub-lished at the end of the eighteenth century and at the beginning of the nineteenth, are powerful, if unpleasant.

Two Southern novelists followed Cooper in dealing with the life of their own neighborhood. One was John Pendle-ton Kennedy (1795–1870), who wrote two Virginia stories, "Swallow Barn," published in 1832, and "Horse-Shoe Rob-inson," published in 1835. The other was William Gilmore Simms (1806–1870), who applied Cooper's method to South-ern scenes and characters; perhaps the most interesting of the many tales due to his facile pen is the "Yemassee," published in 1835.

Although not to be classed as fiction, two books published in the first half of the nineteenth century have all the fas-cination of Cooper's sea stories. One of these is the "Typee" of Herman Melville (1819–1891), in which the author described the strange adventures of a sailor in the

South Seas who was a captive of the natives on one of the Marquesas Islands. The other of these romantic narratives of the ocean is the "Two Years before the Mast" of Richard H. Dana (1815–1882), which has been called the most truthful account of the everyday life of the American sailor that has ever been written. Bryant declared it to be "as good as ' Robinson Crusoe.' "

Certain of the woman writers of the United States have attained distinction as poets and as novelists. The earliest of them was Mrs. Rowson (1762–1824), who wrote the pathetic tale of "Charlotte Temple"; and among the latest were Mrs. Jackson (1831–1885) and Miss Woolson (1848–1894). Mrs. Jackson wrote many books in prose and verse, but she is best known by her moving appeal for the Indian — an appeal cast in the form of a story and called "Ramona." Miss Woolson was a grand-niece of Cooper's and she had not a little of his skill in setting down on paper the impression of natural scenery ; her most artistic books are, perhaps, the two volumes of short stories, in one of which she studied life in the South, and in the other of which she depicted the people who dwell on the shores of the great lakes.

Margaret Fuller (1810–1850) was what very few women have ever trained themselves to be ; she was a critic, having high ideals both of life and of literature. She was a friend of Emerson's and helped to edit the *Dial;* and she was a visitor to Brook Farm, while Hawthorne and Curtis and Ripley were there. She died in her prime, being shipwrecked off Fire Island as she was returning from Europe with her baby and her husband, an Italian named Ossoli.

A woman was also the author of the American book which has had the widest circulation both at home and abroad, both in the English and in translations into foreign languages. Perhaps to-day on the continent of Europe "Uncle Tom's Cabin" is better known than any other single book of American authorship. It was written by Mrs. Harriet Beecher Stowe, who was born in Connecticut in 1812. As a girl she taught school in Cincinnati and had many opportunities of studying Southern life. She married Mr. Stowe in 1836 and moved with him to Maine in 1850, when he was called to a professorship at Bow-

Harriet Beecher Stowe

doin — the college where Hawthorne and Longfellow had graduated. She had a deep feeling against slavery and she thought that everybody would agree with her if only the results of the evil system were understood.

What she tried to do in "Uncle Tom's Cabin" was not to attack slavery but rather to tell the truth about it, so that others would see it as she saw it. She sought to show the good side as well as the bad side; she described the good slave owner and the bad slave owner; she depicted the good slave and the bad slave. She was so free from any hatred of the slave owner himself that the pleasantest character in the book is St. Clair, the charming Southern gentleman, while the coarsest figure of all is the brutal Northern slave driver Legree. It was the system she detested and not the men and women who might be involved in it. This wish to be truthful it is which gives its abiding value to "Uncle Tom's Cabin" and which has obtained for it a life far longer than that of other "novels with a purpose," wherein there is no attempt to set down the facts as they are and let these speak for themselves.

QUESTIONS. — Mention three writers who aided powerfully with their pens the movement for the independence of the English colonies in the New World.

Who were the three public men who did equal service in shaping public opinion in favor of the formation of a strong national government?

What two other public men, in later years, insisted mightily, by word and by deed, upon the necessity of preserving the American Union forever?

Describe some of the work of three famous American historians.

Mention two American essayists who were associated with Hawthorne in the Brook Farm experiment.

Why are the names of Willis and Taylor remembered?

What do you know about Walt Whitman?                           .

What part has the South taken in the production of American literature?

What did Margaret Fuller do?

Discuss the life and work of the most distinguished authoress as yet produced by the Western World.

NOTE. — Biographies of Jefferson, Morris, Hamilton, Jay, Madison, Webster, and Lincoln will be found in the American Statesmen series.

Biographies of Curtis, Ripley, Motley, Willis, Margaret Fuller, Bayard Taylor, and Simms will be found in the American Men of Letters series.

For a Southern criticism of Mrs. Stowe's story, see the *Sewanee Review* for November, 1893.

# XVIII THE END OF THE NINETEENTH CENTURY

THE death of Holmes in the fall of 1894, following fast upon the deaths of Whittier and of Parkman and of Lowell, marked the close of an epoch. The leaders of the great New England group of authors had gone ; and the period of American literature which they had made illustrious was completed. In the first half of the nineteenth century the literary center of the United States had been in New York, where were Irving and Cooper, Bryant, Halleck, and Drake. Toward the middle of the century the literary center had shifted to Boston, in which city or in its immediate vicinity were the homes of Emerson, Longfellow, Whittier, Holmes, Parkman, Lowell, and Thoreau. When these had departed they left no successors there of the same relative influence. The nation has been spreading so fast and the men of letters are so scattered, that there is in the last years of the nineteenth century no single group of authors whose position at the head of American literature is beyond question.

Although there have never been so many authors as there are to-day, and although the average of literary skill is probably higher than ever before, there is now no towering figure and no dominating personality. And those who are at the head of American literature at the end of the nineteenth century are not men of the same general type as the greatly-gifted New Englanders whom they succeeded ; and their aims and their ideals are not the same. They have not the binding tie of birth in the same part of the country, for they come from the South and from the

West as well as from the East.   In so far as the nation
has any literary center, this must be New York again,
although there is no common bond of union among the
many prominent authors living in the metropolis.
After the death of Lowell and Whittier and Holmes
there was left no poet having, as they all three had, at
once a high standing and a wide popularity.   Poets there
are of lofty aspiration and of delicate skill.   Other writers of verse there are also who rimed adroitly the common things of life, using the common speech of the people of their own State.   The praise of those best qualified
to judge has been given rather to the poets of the first of
these groups, while it is the verses of the writers of the
second group which have been most warmly welcomed by
the people as a whole.

Here we find the most marked difference between the
poetry of the middle of the century and that of the end.
The best poems of Longfellow and Whittier delighted all
classes of Americans ; they pleased the plain people as
well as the more highly cultivated.   "Evangeline" and
"Snow-Bound" charmed alike the farmhand and the college professor.   But no long poem published in the last
years of the nineteenth century has achieved this double
distinction.   Of course such a poem may appear at any
moment, but with the increasing vogue of fiction, poetry
seems less preëminent than it was in the past.   Fifty
years ago nearly all the writers who stood at the head of
American literature were poets.   Of the writers who
stand at the head of American literature to-day less than
half are poets.

There is no dearth of poetry ; indeed, it has never been
so abundant in America as it is to-day.   Nor is there any
falling off in its quality, for never has the accomplishment

of verse been possessed by more writers. But perhaps
fame is not now won so swiftly by a beautiful lyric as it
is by a striking short story. Therefore the ambitious
young author is less tempted to confine himself to verse
than he was half a century ago. Fiction is the form of
literature in which many of the leading American authors
at the end of the nineteenth century find their natural
medium of expression. Both the novel and the short
story flourish now as never before.

Two of the more recent developments of fiction are
especially noteworthy. The first of these is what has
been called the "international novel." This name has
been given to a study of American character seen against
a foreign background. To bring out the difference between the American and the European — and more particularly the profound difference between the American
and the Englishman — this has been the object of not
a few novels written by American authors. By making
this contrast these novelists performed a most useful service, for they helped us to see our-
selves as others see us. They forced
us to look at ourselves with alien
eyes. They compelled us to recognize some of our own peculiarities to
which we had chosen to be blind.

Closely akin in method to the international novels have been certain
novels of city life. In these stories
the complex conditions of society in
New York, in Boston, and in Chicago

William D. Howells

have been studied with conscientious care. Certain aspects
of the kaleidoscopic cosmopolitanism of the great cities of
the East have been seized by the novelist and by him so

presented in his stories that the dweller on the lonely farm
in the distant West is enabled to comprehend better than
before the conditions of life amid the shifting scenes of
the mighty city.   This, indeed, is the greatest service the
art of fiction can render to mankind ; it helps us to understand our fellow-man ; it explains us to ourselves.

To perform this service adequately, the aim of the

novelist must be to tell the truth about
life as he sees it.   The aim of the
greatest writers of fiction has not been
merely to amuse by fanciful and fantas-
tic tales, but to interpret sympathetically the life they themselves best knew.
This is what has been done with remarkable success by the authors who
have taken part in the second of the
two recent and noteworthy developments of American fiction.

Edmund C. Stedman

Quite as interesting as the "international novel" is
the "local short story."   By this is meant the story in
which we find set forth the people and the scenery and
the dialect of a particular locality — in which there is
a strong local flavor and a free use of local color.   "Rip Van
Winkle" is the first tale of this type, in which there is
a sympathetic study of the manners and customs of a
special portion of our vast and mingled population.

The example set by Irving has been followed by writers
who happened to have special knowledge of this or that
portion of the country, until there is now hardly a corner
of the United States which has not served as the scene
of a story of some sort.   Many of these local fictions
are short stories, but some of them are long novels.   As
was natural, New England is the portion which has

been most carefully explored.   But of late the young writers of the South and of the West have been almost more suc-cessful in this department of literature than the writers of New England and of New York.   In story and in sketch we have had made known to us the Southern gentleman of the old school, the old negro body-servant, the fieldhand, and the poor white.   In like manner we have had faith-fully observed and honestly presented to us the more marked types of Western character.   What gives its real value to these studies of life in the South and in

Edward Eggleston

the West is that they *are* studies of life, that they have the note of sincerity and of reality, that they are not vain imaginings merely, but the result of an earnest effort to see life as it is and to tell the truth about it — the whole truth, and nothing but the truth.

Samuel Clemens (" Mark Twain ")

Many of these Southern and Western tales, even more than the New York and New England tales on which they are modeled, abound in humor, which some-times refines itself into delicate character - drawing, and which sometimes breaks out into more hearty fun.   Franklin was perhaps the earliest of American humor-ists ; after him came Irving, and then Lowell ; and they have to-day many followers not un-worthy of them.

The earlier American historians, Prescott and Motley and Parkman, have also many not unworthy followers, working to-day as loyally as did their great predecessors. At no time since the United States became an independent nation has there been greater interest in historical study. At no time have more able writers been devoting themselves to the history of our own country.

Although we have now no essayist of the stimulating force of Emerson, and no critic with the insight and the equipment of Lowell, yet there is no lack of delightful essayists and of accomplished critics. Indeed, the general level of American criticism has been immensely raised since the days of Poe. American critics are far more self-reliant at the end of the nineteenth century than they were at the beginning. They have lost the colonial attitude, for they no longer look for light across the Atlantic to England only. They know now that American literature has to grow in its own way and of its own accord. Yet they are not so narrow as they were, and they are ready to apply far higher standards. An American poet or novelist or historian is not now either unduly praised or unduly condemned merely because he is an American. He is judged on his own merits, and he is compared with the leading contemporary writers of England and of France, of Germany, of Italy, and of Spain. It is by the loftiest standards of the rest of the world that American literature must hereafter be measured.

QUESTIONS. — Discuss the shifting of the literary center in the United States during the last quarter of the century.

What marked difference is to be found between the poetry of the middle of the century and that of the end?

What is meant by the "international novel"?

What is meant by the "local short story"?

What is it that now gives abiding value to the best American fiction?

What is the present state of American literature in the departments of history and criticism?

# A BRIEF CHRONOLOGY

# AMERICAN LITERATURE

———•———

1607 . . . John Smith explored the Chesapeake Bay.
Landing at Jamestown, April 26.

1608 . . . John Smith: "A True Relation of Such Occurrences and
Accidents of Note as hath Happened in Virginia."
Quebec founded.

1613 . . . Anne Bradstreet born.

1616 . . . John Smith: "A Description of New England."

1620 . . . Landing of the Pilgrims.

1624 . . . John Smith (with others): "The General History of Virginia, New England, and the Summer Isles."

1636 . . . Harvard College founded.

1639 . . . Increase Mather born.

1640 . . . Richard Mather, John Eliot, and other Chief Divines in
the Country : "The Whole Book of Psalms Faithfully
Translated into English Metre." (The Bay Psalm
Book.)

1650 . . . Anne Bradstreet: "The Tenth Muse lately Sprung up in
America."

1661 . . . John Eliot: Translation of the New Testament into Algon-
quin.

1663 . . . Cotton Mather born.

1672 . . . Anne Bradstreet died.

1689 . . . Cotton Mather : "Memorable Providences relating to
Witchcrafts and Possessions."

1691 . . . Joshua Scottow: "The New England Primer."

1700 . . . Yale College founded.

1702 . . . Cotton Mather: "Magnalia Christi Americana."

1703 . . . Jonathan Edwards born.

1704 . . . *The Boston News-Letter* established.

1706 . . . Benjamin Franklin born.

1710 . . . Cotton Mather: "Bonifacius; an Essay upon the Good that is to be Devised and Designed."

1719 . . . *The Boston Gazette* established.

1721 . . . James Franklin: *The New England Courant.*

1723 . . . Increase Mather died.

1728 . . . Cotton Mather died.

1732 . . . Franklin: "Poor Richard's Almanack."

1737 . . . Thomas Paine born.

1743 . . . Thomas Jefferson born.

1745 . . . John Jay born.

1746 . . . Princeton College founded.

1749 . . . University of Pennsylvania founded.

1750 . . . Franklin: "Hypothesis for Explaining the Several Phenomena of Thunder Gusts; Opinions and Conjectures Concerning the Properties and Effects of the Electrical Matter."

1751 . . . James Madison born.

1752 . . . Gouverneur Morris born.

1754 . . . Jonathan Edwards: "Freedom of the Will." King's College founded — now Columbia College.

1757 . . . Alexander Hamilton born.

1758 . . . Franklin: "Father Abraham's Speech." Jonathan Edwards died.

1762 . . . Mrs. Rowson born.

1764 . . . College of Rhode Island founded — now Brown.

1769 . . . Dartmouth College founded.

1771 . . . Franklin: First five chapters of "Autobiography" written.
Charles Brockden Brown born.

1776 . . . Jefferson: "The Declaration of Independence."
Paine: "Common Sense."

1782 . . . First English Bible published in America (at Philadelphia).
Daniel Webster born.

1783 . . . Washington Irving born.

1787 . . . Jefferson: "Notes on the State of Virginia."

1788 . . . Hamilton (with Madison and Jay): "The Federalist."

1789 . . . Franklin: "Autobiography" from 1757 to 1759 (written).
James Fenimore Cooper and Jared Sparks born.

1790 . . . Fitz-Greene Halleck born.
Franklin died.

1794 . . . William Cullen Bryant born.

1795 . . . Lindley Murray: "English Grammar."
Joseph Rodman Drake and John P. Kennedy born.

1796 . . . Prescott born.

1800 . . . Daniel Webster: "Fourth of July Speech."
George Bancroft born.

1802 . . . Bowdoin College founded.
George Ripley born.

1803 . . . Ralph Waldo Emerson born.

1804 . . . Hawthorne born.
Hamilton died.

1806 . . . Noah Webster: "Compendious Dictionary of the English
Language."
Nathaniel P. Willis and William Gilmore Simms born.

1807 . . . Henry W. Longfellow and John G. Whittier born.

1808 . . . Bryant: "The Embargo."

1809 . . . Irving: "History of New York by Diedrich Knickerbocker."
Paine died.

✗1809 . . . Oliver Wendell Holmes, Abraham Lincoln, and Edgar Allan
Poe born.

1810 . . . Margaret Fuller born.
Charles Brockden Brown died.

1812 . . . Harriet Beecher (Stowe) born.

1814 . . . Motley born.

1815 . . . Richard H. Dana born.

1816 . . . Drake: " The Culprit Fay."
J. G. Saxe born.
Gouverneur Morris died.

✗1817 . . . Bryant: "Thanatopsis " (in the *North American Review*).
Thoreau born.

1819 . . . Drake and Halleck : " The Croaker Poems."
Herman Melville born.
Irving: " The Sketch Book."
James Russell Lowell, Walt Whitman, and ? P. Whipple
born.

1820 . . . Cooper: " Precaution."
Drake died.

1821 . . . Bryant: " Poems."
Cooper: " The Spy."
Richard Grant White born.

1822 . . . Irving: " Bracebridge Hall."
Ulysses S. Grant born.

1823 . . . Cooper: " The Pilot," and " The Pioneers."
Francis Parkman born.

1824 . . . Irving: " Tales of a Traveler."
George W. Curtis born.
Mrs. Rowson died.

1825 . . . Webster: " First Bunker Hill Oration."
Bayard Taylor born.

1826 . . . Cooper: " The Last of the Mohicans."
Jefferson died.

1827 . . . Cooper: "The Prairie."
           Poe: "Tamerlane and Other Poems."

1829 . . . Cooper: "The Wept of Wish-ton-wish," and "The Red
               Rover."
           Irving: "The Conquest of Granada."
           Henry Timrod born.
           Poe: "Al Aaraaf, Tamerlane, and Minor Poems."
           Jay died.

1830 . . . Cooper: "The Water Witch."
           Webster: "Reply to Haynes."

1831 . . . Irving: "The Companions of Columbus."
           Whittier: "Legends of New England."
           Helen Fiske (Hunt Jackson) born.

1832 . . . Irving: "The Alhambra."
           Sparks: "Life of Gouverneur Morris."
           Kennedy: "Swallow Barn."

1833 . . . Longfellow: "Outre-Mer."
           Whittier: "Justice and Expediency."
           Louisa M. Alcott and Edmund C. Stedman born.

1834 . . . Bancroft: "History of the United States."
           Jared Sparks: "Life of Washington."

1835 . . . Simms: "The Yemassee."
           Willis: "Pencilings by the Way."
           Samuel L. Clemens born.
           Kennedy: "Horse-Shoe Robinson."

1836 . . . Emerson: "Nature."
           Holmes: "Poems."
           Madison died.

1837 . . . Hawthorne: "Twice-Told Tales" (first series).
           Prescott: "Reign of Ferdinand and Isabella."
           Emerson: Address on the "American Scholar."
           John Burroughs, Edward Eggleston, and William D. Howells
               born.

1838 . . . Holmes: Boylston Prize Dissertations for 1836 and 1837.
           Lowell: "Class Poem."

1838 . . Poe: "The Narrative of Arthur Gordon Pym."
Whittier: "Ballads and Antislavery Poems."

1839 . . . Cooper: "History of the Navy of the United States."
Longfellow: "Hyperion," and "Voices of the Night."
Bret Harte born.

1840 . . . Cooper: "The Pathfinder."
R. H. Dana, Jr.: "Two Years before the Mast."
Poe: "Tales of the Grotesque and the Arabesque."
Brook Farm Community established.

1841 . . . Cooper: "The Deerslayer."
Emerson: "Essays" (first series).
Longfellow: "Ballads and Other Poems."
Lowell: "A Year's Life."
Poe: "The Murders in the Rue Morgue."
University of Michigan opened.

1842 . . . Bryant: "The Fountain and Other Poems."
Cooper: "The Two Admirals," and "Wing-and-Wing."
. Holmes: "Homeopathy and its Kindred Delusions."
Hawthorne: "Twice-Told Tales" (second series).
Longfellow: "Poems on Slavery."
Sidney Lanier born.
Simms: "Beauchampe."
John Fiske born.

1843 . . . Longfellow: "The Spanish Student."
Prescott: "History of the Conquest of Mexico."
Poe: "The Gold Bug."
Whittier: "Lays of My Home and Other Poems."
Webster: "Second Bunker Hill Oration."

1844 . . . Emerson: "Essays" (second series).
Lowell: "A Legend of Brittany."
Margaret Fuller: "Woman in the Nineteenth Century."

1845 . . . Lowell: "Conversations on Some of the Old Poets."
Poe: "The Raven and Other Poems."

1846 . . . Hawthorne: "Mosses from an Old Manse."
Holmes: "Urania."
Longfellow: "The Belfry of Bruges and Other Poems."

1846 . . . Emerson: " Poems."
Melville: " Typee."
Bayard Taylor: " Views Afoot."
Poe: " The Bells."

1847 . . . Longfellow: " Evangeline."
Melville: " Omoo."
Prescott: " History of the Conquest of Peru."
Whittier: " The Supernaturalism of New England."

1848 . . . Lowell: " The Biglow Papers " (first series); " A Fable
for Critics," and " The Vision of Sir Launfal."
Poe: " Eureka, a Prose Poem."
Whipple: " Essays and Reviews."
Constance Fenimore Woolson and Hjalmar Hjorth Boyesen
born.

1849 . . . Emerson: " Miscellanies."
Irving: " Goldsmith."
Longfellow: " Kavanagh."
Parkman: " The Oregon Trail."
Thoreau: " A Week on the Concord and Merrimac Rivers."
Whipple: " Literature and Life."
Whittier: " Voices of Freedom."
Poe died.

1850 . . . Bryant: " Letters of a Traveler."
Emerson: " Representative Men."
Hawthorne: " The Scarlet Letter."
Irving: " Life of Mahomet and his Successors."
Longfellow: " The Seaside and the Fireside."
Donald G. Mitchell: " Reveries of a Bachelor."
Whittier: " Songs of Labor."
Margaret Fuller died.

1851 . . . Curtis: " Nile Notes of a Howadji."
Hawthorne: " The House of the Seven Gables," " A Wonder-
Book for Boys and Girls."
Longfellow: " The Golden Legend."
Parkman: " History of the Conspiracy of Pontiac."
Cooper died.

✗ 1852 . . . Hawthorne: "The Blithedale Romance," and "The Snow Image and Other Twice-Told Tales."
Harriet Beecher Stowe: "Uncle Tom's Cabin."
Daniel Webster died.

1853 . . . Curtis: "The Potiphar Papers."
Hawthorne: "Tanglewood Tales for Boys and Girls."

1854 . . . Thoreau: "Walden."

1855 . . . Irving: "Life of Washington" and "Wolfert's Roost."
Longfellow: "Hiawatha."
Whitman: "Leaves of Grass."

1856 . . . Curtis: "Prue and I."
Emerson: "English Traits."
Motley: "The Rise of the Dutch Republic."

1858 . . . Holmes: "The Autocrat of the Breakfast Table."
Longfellow: "The Courtship of Miles Standish."

1859 . . . Bryant: "Letters from Spain and Other Countries."
Irving and Prescott died.

1860 . . . Emerson: "The Conduct of Life."
Hawthorne: "The Marble Faun."
Motley: "United Netherlands."
Stedman: "Poems, Lyric and Idyllic."
Whittier: "Home Ballads."
Holmes: "The Professor at the Breakfast Table."

1861 . . . Holmes: "Elsie Venner," and "Songs in Many Keys."

1862 . . . Pierre M. Irving: "Life and Letters of Washington Irving."
Thoreau died.

✗ 1863 . . . Bryant: "Thirty Poems."
Hawthorne: "Our Old Home."
Higginson: "Out-Door Papers."
Thoreau: "Excursions."
Longfellow: "Tales of a Wayside Inn."
Whittier: "In War Time."
Lincoln: "Gettysburg Oration."
Holmes: "Soundings from the Atlantic."

1864 . . . Lowell: "Fireside Travels."
Stedman: "Alice of Monmouth."
Thoreau: "The Maine Woods."
Hawthorne died.

1865 . . . Parkman: "Pioneers of France in the New World."
Thoreau: "Cape Cod."
Lincoln died.

1866 . . . Howells: "Venetian Life."
Thoreau: "A Yankee in Canada."
Whittier: "Snow-Bound."
Jared Sparks died.

1867 . . . S. L. Clemens: "The Celebrated Jumping Frog."
Holmes: "The Guardian Angel."
Howells: "Italian Journeys."
Lanier: "Tiger Lilies."
Longfellow: Translation of Dante.
Lowell: "The Biglow Papers" (second series).
Whittier: "The Tent on the Beach."
Parkman: "The Jesuits in North America."
Halleck, Willis, and Timrod died.

1868 . . . Louisa M. Alcott: "Little Women."
Hawthorne: "Passages from American Notebooks."
Longfellow: "The New England Tragedies."
Whittier: "Among the Hills."

1869 . . . Aldrich: "The Story of a Bad Boy."
Bryant: "Letters from the East."
S. L. Clemens: "Innocents Abroad."
Lowell: "Under the Willows," and "The Cathedral."
Parkman: "La Salle."
Stedman: "The Blameless Prince."
Harriet Beecher Stowe: "Old Town Folks."

1870 . . . Bryant: Translation of the "Iliad."
Emerson: "Society and Solitude."
Bret Harte: "The Luck of Roaring Camp."
Hawthorne: "English Notebooks."

1870 . . . Lowell: "Among My Books."
   Bayard Taylor: Translation of the first part of "Faust."
   Charles Dudley Warner: "My Summer in a Garden."
   Whitman: "Democratic Vistas."
   Whittier: "Miriam," and "Ballads of New England."
   J. P. Kennedy and W. G. Simms died.

1871 . . . Louisa M. Alcott: "Little Men."
   Burroughs: "Wake-Robin."
   Eggleston: "The Hoosier Schoolmaster."
   Hawthorne: "French and Italian Notebooks."
   Higginson: "Atlantic Essays."
   Howells: "Their Wedding Journey."
   Longfellow: "The Divine Tragedy."
   Lowell: "My Study Windows."

1872 . . . S. L. Clemens: "Roughing It."
   Holmes: "The Poet at the Breakfast Table."
   Longfellow: "Three Books of Song."
   Charles Dudley Warner: "Back-log Studies."
   Whittier: "The Pennsylvania Pilgrim."

1873 . . . Aldrich: "Marjorie Daw."
   Bryant: "Orations and Addresses."
   E. E. Hale: "In His Name."
   Howells: "A Chance Acquaintance."

1874 . . . Holmes: "Songs of Many Seasons."
   Howells: "A Foregone Conclusion."
   Longfellow: "Aftermath," and "The Hanging of the Crane."
   Motley: "John of Barneveld."
   Parkman: "The Old Régime in Canada."
   Whittier: "Hazel Blossoms," and "Mabel Martin."

1875 . . . Burroughs: "Winter Sunshine."
   Emerson: "Letters and Social Aims."
   Higginson: "Young Folks' History of the United States."
   Longfellow: "The Masque of Pandora."
   W. T. Sherman: "Memoirs."
   Stedman: "Victorian Poets."

1876 . . . S. L. Clemens: "Tom Sawyer."
Sidney Lanier: "Poems."
Lowell: "Three Memorial Poems."
Johns Hopkins University opened.

1877 . . . Burroughs: "Birds and Poets."
Parkman: "Count Frontenac."
Motley died.

1878 . . . Holmes: "Motley."
James: "French Poets and Novelists."
Longfellow: "Keramos."
Tyler: "A History of American Literature."
Whittier: "The Vision of Echard."
Emerson: Lecture on the Fortune of the Republic
Bryant and Bayard Taylor died.

1879 . . . Boyesen: "Goethe and Schiller."
Burroughs: "Locusts and Wild Honey."
Cable: "Old Creole Days."
Howells: "The Lady of the Aroostook."
James: "An International Episode."
Stockton: "Rudder Grange."

1880 . . . Aldrich: "The Stillwater Tragedy."
Cable: "The Grandissimes."
Joel Chandler Harris: "Uncle Remus."
Holmes: "The Iron Gate."
Howells: "The Undiscovered Country."
Longfellow: "Ultima Thule."
Lew Wallace: "Ben-Hur."
George Ripley died.

1881 . . . Burroughs: "Pepacton."
Whittier: "The King's Missive."
Sidney Lanier died.

1882 . . . S. L. Clemens: "The Prince and the Pauper."
F. Marion Crawford: "Mr. Isaacs."
Howells: "A Modern Instance."
Longfellow: "In the Harbor."

1882 . . . Lounsbury: "James Fenimore Cooper."
Emerson, Longfellow, and R. H. Dana died.

1883 . . . S. L. Clemens: "Life on the Mississippi."
Park Godwin: "Bryant."
Longfellow: "Michael Angelo."
J. Whitcomb Riley: "The Old Swimmin'-Hole."
Whittier: "The Bay of Seven Islands."
Holmes: "Pages from an Old Volume of Life," and "Medical Essays."

1884 . . . H. C. Bunner: "Airs from Arcady."
Cable: "The Creoles of Louisiana."
S. L. Clemens: "Huckleberry Finn."
Helen Hunt Jackson: "Ramona."
Higginson: "Margaret Fuller Ossoli."
Holmes: "Emerson."
Parkman: "Montcalm and Wolfe."
Stockton: "The Lady or the Tiger."

1885 . . . U. S. Grant: "Personal Memoirs."
Howells: "The Rise of Silas Lapham."
Holmes: "A Mortal Antipathy."
Stedman: "Poets of America."
Woodberry: "Edgar Allan Poe."
U. S. Grant, Richard Grant White, and Helen Hunt Jackson died.

1886 . . . Frances Hodgson Burnett: "Little Lord Fauntleroy."
Burroughs: "Signs and Seasons."
Lowell: "Democracy and Other Addresses."
Whipple died.

1887 . . . Cabot: "Memoir of Ralph Waldo Emerson."
F. Marion Crawford: "Saracinesca."
Holmes: "Our Hundred Days in Europe."
McMaster: "Franklin as a Man of Letters."
Thomas Nelson Page: "In Ole Virginia."
Carl Schurz: "Henry Clay."
Stedman: "Library of American Literature."
Mary E. Wilkins: "A Humble Romance."
J. G. Saxe died.

1888 . . . Eggleston : "A History of the United States."
Holmes : " Before the Curfew."
James : "Partial Portraits."
Lowell : " Political Essays."
Riley : "Old-Fashioned Roses."
Louisa M. Alcott died.

1889 . . . Burroughs : "Indoor Studies."
Howells : " A Hazard of New Fortunes."
Lodge : "Washington."
Roosevelt : "The Winning of the West."

1890 . . . Holmes : "Over the Teacups."
Mahan : "The Influence of Sea-Power upon History."
Nicolay and Hay : "Abraham Lincoln."

1891 . . . Eggleston : "The Faith Doctor."
Fiske : " The American Revolution."
Garland : " Main-traveled Roads."
Howells : " Criticism and Fiction."
Lowell : "Latest Literary Essays."
Barrett Wendell : " Cotton Mather."
Bancroft, Lowell, and Melville died.

1892 . . . Boyesen : " Essays on German Literature."
Fiske : " The Discovery of America."
Lowell : "The Old English Dramatists."
Thomas Nelson Page : " The Old South."
Parkman : "A Half Century of Conflict."
Stedman : " The Nature and Elements of Poetry."
Trent : "William Gilmore Simms."
Whittier : "At Sundown."
G. W. Curtis, Whittier, and Whitman died.
University of Chicago opened.

1893 . . . G. W. Curtis : "Orations and Addresses."
Fuller : " The Cliff Dwellers."
Barrett Wendell : " Stelligeri."
Parkman died.

1894 . . . Clemens : " Pudd'nhead Wilson."
Warner : " The Golden House."

1894 . . . Mary E. Wilkins: "Pembroke."
Holmes and Constance Fenimore Woolson died.

1895 . . . Fuller: "With the Procession."
Howells: "My Literary Passions."
Roosevelt and Lodge: "Hero Tales of American History "
Stockton: "Captain Horn."
Boyesen died.

1896 . . . Harriet Beecher Stowe died.

# INDEX

---

www.ingramcontent.com/pod-product-compliance
Lightning Source LLC
Chambersburg PA
CBHW030645030726
47497CB00006B/1959